DUSK

Reilly Smith

FIRST WINBURN STUDIOS EDITION, JANUARY 2019

Library of Congress Cataloging-in-Publication Data is available upon request.

First Winburn Studios Paperback ISBN: 978-1-7335421-0-4

Cover Design by Katherine Smith

Author Photo by John Jefferson

Printed in the United States of America

10 9 8 7 6 5 4 3 2 1

for Katie

EDITOR'S NOTE

The following is an account taken from the collective writings of John Durban and Sam Winburn that spanned more than four years, from August 29, 2006 to October 4, 2010. According to our research, the dates mentioned in their chronicling are valid. As far as we know, the events portrayed are true and accurate.

Illustrations intended to be inserted within the text were never received. Their descriptions and placements have been left unaltered.

Part One

PARIS
August 30, 2006

Yesterday I turned twenty-five. The sun was setting on the lawn beneath the Eiffel Tower and I was alone, waiting for its lights to spark. There was a book by my side – Hunter Thompson's *Fear and Loathing*, also an open bottle of cheap Bordeaux, a good roll of camembert and a rumored baguette I had earlier picked up at Le Pain d'Epi. In those last quiet moments, I felt distraught and living inside of a guidebook or postcard, preserving solitude before a stumbling figure appeared in the corner of my eye. I watched him lap surrounding paths in the short, staggered walk of a controlled belligerent, and waited. Aside from his appearance, which was pristine and tailored, he was moving with an authority I'd never before witnessed, as if belonging to a man so far beyond composure, there was no naming it. At once, he made approach. I conjured everything to appear frigid and unapproachable.

John Durban sat close enough I could feel him breathing. The center of his eyes appeared in riot, a fleeting vitality. The first tones in his voice were bitter and dragging, but cool, not heavy. His hair was unkempt and thrown about a beautiful, caramel-toned face. I would have let everything ride on his seeing neither a mirror nor honest sleep in a month. Within seconds of his arrival, I was too haunted to escape. He began to form sentences and thoughts in a drawl that seemed foreign English, as I remember having to initially cope with understanding him one word at a time. Then he was putting his lips on my wine and drinking it hard, tearing hunks of the precious bread and using it to also tear through the camembert, all while ranting about some claimed conspiracy within the French government. I began to figure acid in his veins, the resulting million holes melting through fibers of his internal body. He was ferocious. Once darkness fell and the Eiffel lit, he finally reached across himself to offer an introduction. I thought there were so many things wrong with him.

I was waiting for two Jap birds that I could fuck with and not speak to. They were the only reason you'd find me in Paris anywhere near the goddamn Eiffel Tower. Burn was sitting alone with his legs crossed, writing in a journal. Fragile and naïve and a fucking bore, I thought. He eventually said it was his twenty-fifth birthday and that he was in Europe to see the world and die. I suppose that changed things a bit. I liked the way he spoke and admired his arrangement of words and thought. He had an odd charm...as if he both adored and despised playing a part in his life at all. I'm an educated man, an Oxford man, worldly and still, I'd never heard anything exactly like him. I took instant note of the softness in his face, the tones in his voice, and determined he was capable enough to invite for an evening out. Especially when my rendezvous didn't show. See, I had been walking alone for quite some time.

INSERT SKETCH: DURBAN AND BURN UNDER THE EIFFEL, SHADOWS, SPARKLE

When Durban arrived, I was in the middle of writing a letter to a girl Naomi back in the States. We had fallen into something I had always refused to categorize in the month preceding my departure from Los Angeles. Durban saw her name as a header on a blank piece of paper and then immediately became obsessed to know everything he could. I spoke to quiet him, words about a girl who had a movement about her that was different and exciting. From the start, I suspected there were also volatile factors behind her movement which would ultimately break us apart. That's why we began. Volatility excited me. She was also physically beautiful, kind, and treated the world as if it needed her care. So, we continued. I can't say exactly and couldn't confirm to Durban why for four weeks I had never wanted or needed someone or something so bad as I needed her. There was no reason why taking her and having her over and again only elevated that need. Or why it suddenly stopped, and I had to get out.

Durban was nodding and saying things like yeah totally bro, but I could tell he wasn't listening. He drifted semi-permanently and made zero effort to mask the state of his attention. I actually took a moment to admire him before he pulled a baby Ziploc from inside his jacket pocket and snorted its contents like a human-head vacuum. From then on, I was his fascination.

She was fucking some other dude. Some bro. Someone unlike him. Someone harder. I knew it the second he spoke. Here's the thing about Burn that's tragic – he's a fool for love. It means if he's leaving to travel the world and meets a girl, his mind will make her the end of an existence…turning her from what she would usually only be, curiosity, into something dangerously bigger. I had known him for minutes and it was obvious that's exactly what he was doing. He said he was in love and that I didn't understand, that I couldn't understand. Because they existed on a plane deeper than anything I could conjure, I'm guessing. Let me be brief, take us back, and recite the intel I had already gathered…

He was madly in love. Madly. That was the most specific and important word he used to describe the days he spent with this girl back in Los Angeles. He knew that at the end of those short days, he was leaving to see the world and die – or so he had already said to me, and hopefully to no one else, because he had said it without irony. She drove him to the airport. To say goodbye. At the airport, on a curb, he had a moment, a choice to stay or a choice to go…a choice to play the

dealt hand or walk from it. He said she was crying, soaking his shoulder and holding his shirt and that every breath of it turned him inside out, tore him apart. But then he walked away and got on a plane and left her standing there. On that curb. People looking at her. Looking at the crying, sad girl, who was alone. He never looked back. What the fuck more would I ever need to know?

We began walking to Durban's hotel because he was insistent I join him for drinks and dinner. He reminded me during points of my hesitation that it was the day of my birth, and that nothing we did that night would be up to me, saying our only choice was to, "Let the fates guide and remove us." He seemed to enjoy considering himself part of something, in this case my birthday, as if tending to it were a point of focus unlike that which he would otherwise be focusing on. I told him things hadn't felt right since touching down in Paris. Not only was Naomi on my mind, but I'd been sleeping in a cheap and shitty hotel on the far end of town. It wasn't at all what I had imagined. Instinct told me to remove myself from Durban then. When I tried to summon the words to separate us, none came.

Place Vendome was lit and the world inside appeared spectacular. I was trying to take it in as Durban kept carrying on about a stop he'd recently made in Moscow to "handle" some seventeen-year-old Mafioso's daughter he may or may not have impregnated. Words were pouring out of him without pause, like he finally had a vehicle through which he could confess his sins. None appeared built around a need or desire to impress. That was interesting to me. He told me "mob goons" forcefully picked him up outside airport customs, threw him into a van, hooded him, and dragged him to the top of one of those pastel cylindrical roofs. There, they hung him from his ankles over a ten-story drop, threatening his life until he pissed his pants and pissed all over his face. The tremble in his voice made me feel like this had all actually happened, and recently.

As we arrived at Ritz Paris, bellhops opened the doors with greeting to Monsieur Durban. Inside the lobby, I soon felt as if anyone who had ever been employed or associated with the hotel was stopping to greet us. Each received a warm and genuine handshake from Durban, many coupled with a large bill. Durban displayed an innate, distinct form of charm. As I watched those passing moments unfold, it was as if the entire collection of his life was without effort being showcased before me. He was easily as grand and impressive as any man I'd known. Jean-Pierre was the name of the general manager. I have a hard time remembering names but remember his exactly, because of the way Durban presented him as an Englishman or American doing a smug French accent. Jean-Pierre shook my hand and kissed my cheek before Durban changed to French and both of them became very serious. Jean-Pierre turned to signal the bellhops, who rushed to meet him. They traded quick French whispers, then darted out the front doors. I remember thinking of how fast-moving and out of control Durban's world was to me when Jean-Pierre reached out and placed his personal card in my hand. He pulled me close with a deliberate, lowered gaze. Through the tops of his eyes, he spoke with tremendous insistence, "For anything Monsieur Burn. Anything."

Durban led me down winding corridors and into Hemingway, where we carved through a tight crowd and sat down onto two seats waiting at the far end of the bar. True to name, the man was everywhere: lurking in portraits on the wall, staring stone-faced through magazine covers. Even random photos were supposedly taken by and inspired through his eyes. Durban winked at the bartender who then dropped two glasses and a half-empty bottle of dark liquor in front of us. I tried to read the label, but it was frayed and faded. If Durban hasn't yet mentioned his relationship with money, perhaps it's best I offer for purposes of this story that he has so much the concept is lost.

I began pointing around the room, mentioning pictures of the famed "Lost Generation." I told him

Hemingway and Fitzgerald used to have drinks in the same seats we were in, that Orson Welles used to walk the halls, Sartre, Chaplin, on and on. He would acknowledge and smile with a hollow excitement, humoring me. He was unaware of the past, so also lacked any of the reverence necessary to understand and appreciate the inestimable moments that had at one time sat before us. Here I was with this person who at times claimed great respect for the written word, who happened to be sitting in one of the world's holy temples of the written word, and yet, he had never read *The Sun Also Rises*. He also didn't know Coco Chanel, who had lived there for some thirty years – not that that's a big fucking deal to know Coco Chanel, but in his case, it should have been. Ritz Paris wasn't some kitsch bunk where masses paid to eat and drink and fuck and sleep. For some one hundred years, it has been centerline on the cultural and artistic vein of Paris, and the world. For someone to overlook something so big so blindly was beyond a disappointment. I nearly fled.

Durban began to resemble a person heavier handed than I had initially hoped. Of course I read Hemingway. In *Gatsby* and *Tender Is the Night*, Fitzgerald mentioned the small Chicago suburb I grew up in. I was aware of what had come before me. But I didn't say anything. Durban just kept talking, until he became more fanatical than admiring – which was probably the drugs. He was doing a lot of them, and out in the open. It was as if he thought he had been born in the wrong stanza of time, and that the best days of the world had escaped him.

Burn took the scotch in slow. I did not. I needed to move. I had met a striking blonde at Hemingway two nights prior. She was from Stockholm, some transient fashion lawyer. In bed she loved a hard, casual fuck. On the night of Burn's birthday, she was in Hemingway again. I thought she was exactly what he needed, consummation of new skin and being. When she approached us, I stood, gave up my seat so she could exist next to Burn. This was the first time her and I had seen each other since our encounter. She was graceful and cool, sipping Cristal with a jetting pinky, enchanting enough for me to reach into Burn's pocket and steal his phone as they talked. I said nothing and left.

Susanna was her name. She and Durban both honed in on a similar thing, that I had left America and Naomi and was still falsely attached to one of them. At first I tried to keep our conversation abstract and impersonal but she persisted, "Why don't you show me your room." That was the last thing on my mind. When the bartender poured beginnings of a '59 Haut Brion, she took a deep breath and exhaled very dramatically, as if to re-route desires. She picked up the bottle and told me I was fortunate to have such fortunate friends. When I mentioned Durban and I had just met, she smiled sweetly. Then she lifted a glass and asked about Naomi. For whatever reason, I spoke to her, perhaps to justify my denial of her advances. Words came out, until my words reduced to a bitter static, every syllable more defeated and less significant than the previous, until I had nothing left to say. Susanna had lit a cigarette and began to drift like Durban, nodding and listening but never actually. I realized there was nothing necessarily wrong with Durban or Susanna's drift, in spite of what I had earlier thought. It was a moment for me. Finally piqued by my silence, she put out her cigarette and said, "Welcome at last. Everything now begins."

I was walking the streets of Paris because stillness kills. Also, I had stolen Burn's phone with intention of making as many long distance calls as it took to sever him from this thing Naomi. I was walking through the French Quarter with a bottle of Lillet in hand, because it felt local, and I was choking it down, admittedly drinking for sport while calling her number over and over, impersonating an animal until she finally picked up. I presented myself as I often do, with forged exclamation before mentioning Paris and the meeting of her man. I spoke my concerns about his current life's direction and then pleaded her to set him free, quickly following up with implications of her infidelity. She of course denied and took offense to these implications. I coolly reminded her of the day, of metaphorical rebirth and otherwise, before she hung up for the first time. I called back. We talked. She hung up again. I called back. We talked. She hung up. It went on like this for some time, my presenting beliefs until these beliefs would become abrasive and likely quite offensive before she would hang up. Looking back, I can't say why she didn't let my calls go to voice mail. So I must give her credit for that, remaining present in the face of such an aggressor. Far more important than any concession I make, however, was that two important things happened during our exchange. Right away I knew, by the breath she took after my first accusation, that I was correct about everything. Also and progressively, I understood that she loved him, maybe even madly. The girl wasn't a monster. Of course not.

I had been sitting alone for fifteen minutes when Durban finally returned. He sat down and asked about Susanna and dinner and the wine, then moved to questions about how we fucked. When I told him nothing happened, he was confused then betrayed then upset. He told me I missed a great opportunity, that beneath her insistent exterior was the dire and rare spirit of a woman whose lessons I desperately needed to learn. In the moments that followed, I felt a rush of regret for having ever mentioned anything about myself to him, or for even looking at him beneath the Eiffel Tower. I demanded he not mention Naomi again, ferocious enough that my words struck. He seemed mindless before a sudden honesty arrived saying, "You'll never amount to anything taking on the world like this. You'll exist to live and die like the rest of them, and be unbothered by it. That's the worst part. You're sad. And disgusting. Sad fucking disgusting coward." In a swift stroke, I reached for and stabbed a steak knife into the wall beside his head. He looked to the knife, then to me, disappointed and said, "Fuck you, I do not recant."

When I met Burn, I remember thinking for certain I could take him, that if anything arose between us, I could put him down. Our first incident made me unsure. The space between us formed a sharp intensity, far beyond anything that had already occurred. It was like we saw each other truly for the first time, right before his stolen cell phone rang from inside my side pocket. I surrendered it. He looked at it and the caller without saying a word. Then, he answered calmly. I was planning to return the phone upon sitting, to remove myself from the equation – of a theft I had committed and its approaching truth, but we were suddenly past that. She began saying things into the phone and I was watching his face, waiting, as a lover of carnage, for all I had already envisioned. Something like this...

Excitement in his eyes. Excitement on his person appearing quickly, vastly before he would excuse himself into the hallway and away from me. I would grab my drink and follow, savoring him, keeping my distance, out of sight but never too far to obstruct myself from his real-time obliteration. I would pity him for moments, for selfish reasons only, perhaps reflecting upon my own inability to connect with something that could obliterate me. At a point in the conversation, he would turn to face me perfectly. I would see everything unfold there, slow motion in my mind, moments inside moments she so bravely told him, where my pride in her would reach beyond explanation, aware of how few would be either willing or able to accept such a role and give freedom like that. For those reasons alone, I would kiss her deeply and rip out her throat. I would fuck her and saw her in half. With my eyes fixed on Burn, I would watch as a seam opened along the front and center of his body, as the whole of his spewing guts emptied onto the marble floor. Judging on parallel and past cases, I would give him a couple thousand dollars and then cut loose. That's what I assumed beforehand – the two of us as anything but enduring. I admit these mistaken visions of his situation now because in reality, when she told him, nothing really happened. Nothing funny or wild or horrific or dramatic. He sat there, and he took everything. Then he said he was sorry. Then he said goodbye. Then, he hung up.

When I was a young kid around eight years old, once or twice a year from December until the end of February, the skies would open up and dump enough snow on Chicago to turn the world white. When word eventually spread that school was cancelled, all the neighborhood kids took to the streets. At the end of my block, on Washington Circle at the crossing of Ryan Place, there was a distinct five-street intersection where all plows from converging blocks would dump their snow into massive piles rising higher than any of the single story homes on the street. Once the plows vanished, my older brother Michael and I would begin excavation on a plot of land, to create a fort that was all and only ours.

Key to building a fort begins with traction in the snow. Loose snow runs the risk of a cave in, or can leave the fort prone to attack from organized marauders. Pack it too tightly and there's little room to adapt or expand into new territory. Michael and I always started our dig on the embankment opposite the street's most obvious and towering pile of snow. We aimed to separate ourselves from the collective.

When digging tunnels in snow, most kids make the mistake of using gloves, to avoid the pain. Michael and I believed, early on, that it was imperative to never use gloves. This particular snow day was a great one, and I remember it so well because when the day was over, a deep sadness came over me. When the fort was complete and we were finished and spent, Michael and I laid down shoulder to shoulder with our backs against the snow. Michael had brought a small FM radio and battled the wheel before settling on "Black." The acoustics of the fort were excellent. All we had left was to stare at the ceiling, to bask in the warmth of our creation. We talked about *Star Wars* and dreams of our own eventual star travel, of the mysteries dominating our young lives. We did this for hours past five o'clock, the time we were supposed to be home for dinner. We should have stayed forever. All we built would become lost.

Burn and I were walking through the Palais Royal and he was swaying in his steps. After speaking with Naomi, he began to drink violently. When he initially mentioned The Louvre, it was almost nine, and I thankfully told him it was closed without feeling like a liar. Not that I have a problem with general lying, but I did when it came to him. Burn was quickly proving himself an exception to my well-established rules. Since we were only a short walk away and had a bit of time to kill, I told him I would be willing to entertain his desires and at least see the outside of it.

I had given Durban the option of leaving me on my own, several times. He made it obvious that The Louvre was not a place he wanted to go, instead offering a range of options that all seemed to center around prestige or prostitution. There was something hanging over us. As human beings, we didn't belong together. I understood how great Durban was at being glancing and how he lacked personal consistency, because I understood myself. And yet, we weren't separating. I kept thinking on these things, especially after we began to prove useless to each other, as our shared events over the course of the night would consist of a constant compromise, beginning with his accommodating my needs and our walking to the world's most famous museum and glut for tourism. I wanted to see and stand in the presence of something that felt significant, even if only from the outside. Durban seemed to have an affected understanding of such a feeling once I spoke it aloud. And so, a layer on him fell. We were walking and a swirl of momentum was building around him, primed to erupt into something distant and poignant before his body and breath muted and I felt as if I was for the first time speaking with actual John Durban. He asked what I thought of Paris. Then, he waited in silence for my response. I told him I thought it was morose and beautiful. He kept walking, saying only, "Continue." I told him the skies hung heavy, like a deterrent for escape. I told him the streets were hypnotic and monochromatic, that the colors existing leapt beautifully because of it, and that I felt a romance in the people in spite of what I was told to expect. He said nothing as I kept talking, until we rounded the corner to find The Louvre alive. Neither one of us knew it was open until 10 on Wednesday nights. He saw this and turned to me with, "There is no way we are entering that monstrosity with one hour to see everything in our present states. I got this cocaine straight from Bolivia that'll work wonders on someone like you, however, we can only do it if I am made to believe all of this was your idea. And I cannot be held responsible for whatever occurs tonight."

Burn mentioned my coke and insisted we use it as a cultural enhancer. The stuff I had came straight from La Paz, uncut unlike everything, everywhere else. It's not that I get off on calling myself a discernable user, but at a certain point, if it doesn't come direct from the jungle, nothing happens. With regards to Burn's involvement in our collaborative drug use, someone important and reverent who I can't remember and don't feel like looking up once said that a man must be torn down completely before he could ever begin to rebuild himself again. That's why I didn't limit Burn's intake, but rather encouraged it beside the gaudy Louvre pyramid, then again inside the immediate WC and gift shop. Then again in sculptures. Then again through drawings and archeological. He was moving quickly

and absorbing everything. I couldn't have cared less about the art that night. Burn embodied it.

The place was cavernous, enormous, opulent, overwhelming. We were trying to cover the entire grounds in an hour because that's all the time we had. At some point before we entered, I was rational enough to realize that returning the following day would mean I could spend all the time I wanted inside, without Durban or the pressure of a ticking clock. I even presented the option to him. He only said, "The world ends tonight." I don't remember where we started, only that I felt incredibly engaged, even as we blew through exhibits. I felt myself gathering energy from the collective, the thousand still works and the thousand people we were constantly ducking and dodging. They were all moving so slowly. We saw *Mona Lisa* from afar. Durban claimed her an unbearable smug and undeserving of our time. We moved quickly, past the statue *Venus de Milo*, *The Coronation of Napoleon*, medieval walls, *Raft of the Medusa*, everything that presented itself as a spectacle in favor of works we didn't have to fight to witness. At one point, Durban inexplicably shot a piece of yellow latex onto the wing of *Nike of Samothrace*. I don't know where he got it from or how it was fired at such a velocity, but the sound of its impact was a great and suctioning thud. Everyone turned and became mortified as security charged in and we shuffled out. Durban said the latex was a deflated children's balloon and that he had no idea it would travel so far and fast. He said he was trying to hit some asshole from across the room. We covered miles in the precious minutes we had. At the end of the night, everything was closing and security had finally caught up with and detained Durban. He was in the process of apologizing to an assistant curator, and within a minute, had turned himself from a threat to the sanctity of The Louvre, into a distinguished patron of high esteem. That's how well he spoke when things became necessary.

The curator's name was Philippe, and once he realized who I was, everything was mostly forgiven.

Once The Louvre was empty, Philippe took us back to a painting that Burn wanted to spend more time with. It had initially brought him to a full stop we couldn't afford. The painting was by a French artist named Jacques-Louis David, and was called *Le Serment des Horaces*, or *Oath of the Horatii*. Once we arrived, I stood back. Philippe stood beside Burn and began fielding questions I couldn't hear. Since Burn refuses to describe the painting because he feels it dishonest of the moment, I must do it. Three Roman brothers, the Horatii, stand on the left frame, swords raised high into the air to meet their father's sword. The painting is a depiction of Roman legend, where the brothers Horatii agreed to fight three brothers Curiatti from Alba to save endless lives and spare war. To the right, a Horatii sister sits weeping on the floor, in anticipation of great sadness having married one of her brother's enemies. At a point, I heard Philippe translating its meaning to Burn. Then Burn said, "So it's about sacrifice." Philippe nodded and added, "But of course. And of course, the unseen tragedy."

We left The Louvre in a cab. Burn seemed more floating than high. I would also say he was liberated. We were on our way to a high-fashion soiree in Pigalle; a launch for some line by Alexander McQueen. There was an expanse of physical beauty everywhere, so unmatched by any other place in the world. Uniquely Parisian. We rode the elevator up with Kate Moss and David Beckham and the entire time, Burn was standing in the corner, half-mumbling and in a state. I was sending him glances, trying to curb him slightly, at least while we were beside company but nothing was settling. Looking back now, I can see how hopeless my efforts must have been – Burn was already aboard a runaway train, hauling deep afflictions I did not know of at the time. I was battling a current to get to him, and the drugs amplified everything. They made the rolling river between us roar. We were doing a lot. And we kept doing more. It was just so fun having him there. At some point, I told Beckham that Burn had a strange heart, but not because of me. A stale moment hung through the space when Burn realized we were talking about him. The doors opened. Beckham stepped aside to let the lady pass and then followed her out. Burn and I surged out together. Two floors of a loft had been cleared with full views of the city, which felt naked and vulnerable beyond the glass. Inside, the service staff and dancers were all nude, only covered by brushes of red paint across their dicks and tits and pussies. They were all so pensive and self-conscious.

I remember blue dicks. They were absurd and everywhere. I remember slamming Champagne and finding myself trapped in conversations. The world was swirling and blaring. I felt desperate need to stop the ride, to jump off, to slow everything down, but Durban purposefully left no exit. I remember a bathroom, the more lines he was cutting that we kept doing, and the two girls who came in with us. I remember us talking briefly before he took one into a stall. I remember the sound of them against the walls. I remember the moment the second girl began licking my neck and demanding I fuck her. I remember feeling sick and apologizing, because I couldn't do it. I remember the stall beside me going silent, and tasting acid on my lips. When I pulled back, the eyes of a scorned 18-year-old looked upon me. They were grappling rejection. That a man would not perform her demands upon the counter of such an impeccable bathroom sink clearly countered any precedent she had known. She turned with a fury, skillfully unlocked the door and moved back into the party. Durban and his began anew. By then I was halfway out.

The truth was, I was worried Burn might bail on me. When my girl realized the absence of my attention, she hit me across the face. I couldn't bother defending myself. She was young and French and wouldn't have

understood the importance of my getting to him, to stand beside what I had deemed his awakening. I watched her storm out, pushing the door with a tiny fist before I took a moment for myself, to compose and reflect in front of the mirror. Her ring and lefty punch had opened a small gash beneath my right eye. A bit of blood had arrived, and ran. I had bled before, and recently, but as my drops fell into the sink and spread across white marble, I felt a new vitality in it. And I felt vitality in the night, and in Burn. With him around, it felt as if I were on a grand adventure, and that grand adventure was on its way.

I stepped back into the party and watched him from darkened corners, always out of sight. For an hour or two, he did nothing in particular. There were several stops at the bar, several conversations, and a couple things he tried to eat. At one point, he brought an older and lonesome behaving woman onto the dance floor. When the song was over, she smiled and kissed him on the cheek and left. It was Grace Coddington. When alone and with nothing to do, he would retreat to the balcony and look out onto the city, staying there for minutes at a time before walking back inside and again finding nothing to do. He never tried to leave.

Five years before Paris, almost to the day, I came home from college and found my brother alone in his room, dead. I've never done heroin so I can't speak to what it is or what it feels like. I can speak to walking into a room and finding an only brother gone from the world. I knew it the moment I saw him. The air was frozen, not cold just still. Outside his windows, the world was bright and sunny, but inside, the room was gray, as if the light was either forbidden or refusing entry. He had pulled the sheets up to his neck and was curled, having turned to face away from the door and the world. All I could see was the silhouette of his back as I softly approached, hopelessly calling his name lightly. When I reached the bed, I sat down, placed my hand on his leg, over the sheet. Then I sat there for hours, waiting for him to move, to return. Mom and Dad were out of town for the week. We would be alone in that house until I decided to give us up.

Michael and I used to read books to each other when we were very young. Since he was two years older than I was, he did most of the reading. He was my best friend. When the drugs started to take hold, I knew. He hid them well from the world, always speaking of the changes he was making and the corners he was turning, but I saw everything. I saw everything and still let him fall. I wanted nothing more than to believe in every good word he spoke. There was one book that was my all time favorite, Margaret Wise Brown's *Goodnight Moon*. It was the first book he ever read to me, the one I look back on and remember carrying to his room constantly, constantly begging him to read it again, again and again, long after I had memorized every word. Something in the colors and the shapes. The beauty of it. I mention it now because *Goodnight Moon* was sitting on his bed stand, next to his body. He had sought it out and pulled it from the depths of our house before he died. And he either read it or just wanted it beside him when things were coming to a close, because I believe he knew. There was a pillow on the far side of the bed. I climbed over him, to put my head on the pillow and to be with him, beside him. Lying there, I felt the fog of the room envelop me. I opened our book and read it aloud, over and over again, through the night, to try and pay back all the times he had read it to me. In the morning, I called 911. Three days later, my 23-year-old brother was put into the ground.

Inside the loft, all that remained of a once decadent party were vampires and pedophiles. I put my drink down on the railing and began to make a path towards the exit when three guys stepped in front of me. They were very pretty, very European with sloppy English and tight leather. They were also looking to settle a score. One with dark hair and a squint stepped forward and accused me of, "Trying to fuck it with girlfriend." I looked behind him, caught the eyes of my failed bathroom conquest and watched her look away. What none of them knew about me, what few could see, was that the years and trials of my life had emptied me of a certain fear. That's not me trying to sound tough. I don't believe I am, or in trying to be. What I am saying is that no matter the state of my mind or the state of my vision, if it's about me or someone else unconscious on a shit-trampled floor, it won't be me.

The knuckles in my right hand curled and gathered hard. The first guy was talking too loud, trying to create a scene when I detached. Then my hand flew. The instant of connection I felt the snap of his jaw. Both broken, and dislodged. I stepped quickly and with my left, cut down the second guy, their biggest. When I looked to the third, he had already stepped back. The room was silent. I came back. I wanted to apologize but couldn't speak. I wanted to erase. Conscious eyes that remained were all staring at me. I couldn't remove my gaze from the damage I had done. Those boys on the floor suddenly looked like children. Dead children on that shitty floor. And I put them there. With tears in my eyes quickly lining my face, I stared through the girl that had delivered us. It was my desperate attempt to transfer even a fraction of the hatred and regret I felt. Of course I kept it all. Durban's sotto voice rolled over my shoulder and into my ear, "I think we're done here."

We walked back to the hotel not saying much, taking our time with the last hour or so of darkness. I'd never really seen anything like what Burn had unleashed on those boys. All I could think of was the softness I had so recently known him to represent. But to be capable of such contradiction, was special. We got up to the room just as the horizon was starting to glow. I had arranged for all of Burn's things to be transferred from his across the town shitbox to my wing at The Ritz. He said very little about it, only that he was hungry so I called down to room service. I sat down on

the bed and watched as he began to pace. He was calming. I was certain of that. I thought maybe he was getting tired enough to sleep for the day when something else happened. He smiled and started to laugh. Then a lightness spread about the room because I felt invited to join in. So I did. It felt like everything we had been through, so much and really nothing at all had cauterized something between us. I was certain Burn was reflecting too. On Europe, his lost Naomi, the party finale. Then out of nowhere, I worried I was in danger, that he might turn on me, take me by the hair and just smash my head into the wall repeatedly until my skull caved in. He didn't.

The food came. I had ordered everything on the menu; so much they had to bring it on four carts. Me and Burn ate, talked in spurts about art, the books we'd read, music, movies. It was comfortable. We were dancing circles around an unspoken understanding that the night was what it was, and we were who we were. There was a significant moment when I asked Burn if he was alright and he said yes, that he was. I'm not sure I believed him.

I woke up the next afternoon in bed at the Ritz, initially disoriented. I remembered a name, John Durban, like it had been branded into my eyelids, like his were the only two words I knew in the world. I immediately thought two things. The first, I never wanted to see him again. The second, I couldn't live without him. I drifted into his side of the suite. It seemed only fitting to find it abandoned.

PRAGUE
September 24, 2006

I woke up one Sunday morning on the hardwood floor of my Boscolo Carlo presidential, covered in cold, rank piss. There was a pounding noise shaking the room. I ditched my pants and opened the door to find the general manager standing with two brutes. He was holding a copy of my bill in his hand, telling me in broken English that my card had been over-extended, and that I was no longer welcome at his establishment. No one seemed to know of or give a shit about my worldly status or of my worldly friends. To them, I was just some broke deadbeat who had recently pissed his pants. I managed to negotiate thirty minutes for a shower and change of clothes, all the while trying to piece together the previous night. I've always found the cold shower to be an excellent avenue for recollection, and right on cue, as those frozen and resurrecting ropes of water hit my face and ran my lengths, everything came back.

The reason I was in Prague...there was a girl. Google is a runaround, as are book lawyers, so I'm just going to call her Girl. She had recently covered Italian Vogue and had a thing for men with deep pockets and vicious addictions. We met when I was in Rome, where she told me to meet her in Prague. While she was in Prague, she was both looking to reconnect with an estranged family and for someone to get her off, and off, and off, and so on. There were few places in the world I would have rather been.

I was at Girl's house, somewhere just outside the city, having dinner with her family. They were serving goulash of some sort – that's what she called it in translation. I remember trying to eat it and my face being so numb from cocaine – we had picked up a half-key on the way over – that I couldn't chew. I put a bite in my mouth and let it sit for what could have been a short time. Or, a long time. Everyone was speaking Czech and fiercely arguing, I think insulted by my being there, some rude high asshole fucking their overnight famous Czech princess. I could see their eyes and feel their tones, not needing to speak their language to know what the conversation was about. The family was well off, and they had found success through things like hard work and study and dedication. Her and I were the opposite of everything they stood for. Theirs was a conservative family of doctors and lawyers and the thought of her jet-setting, posing famously with her hand not covering her pussy, and shaking up with a creature such as myself eased no collective heart. In spite of my charm, which often appears bottomless, theirs is the breed that sees through me. Looking back, I have no idea what we were doing there. The whole experience was grotesque. Maybe she wanted to smear her success in their faces, I don't know. On several occasions, Girl's father had to step between her and her two brothers because they were threatening physical harm to me or to her or to both of us, I don't know. What I did know was that if they did touch her, or me, I was going to stab out their eyes and hearts with my goulash knife. Not because I cared for her necessarily, or because I felt a need to defend her, but more because I liked the idea of these things, of chivalry, of masquerading as a guy who defends the honor of a girl whose name I should have known but did not.

When I tried to swallow the goulash, it got caught in my throat. I began choking and violently. My body, fueled by the drugs, began a thrash about the room. Girl's two brothers picked me up and tried to save me with some crude form of Czech Heimlich. One of them was balancing me over the back of a chair while the other was lifting my legs and punching my spine.

Before I had any opportunity to object, the goulash shot out of my throat and iced our dessert, a brick of Mom's homemade fruitcake. I was getting my composure, rising to thank the brothers and to break a bottle of wine over their brick-shaped heads when I saw Girl's father holding our bag of cocaine. I had been wearing it in my crotch, apparently too loosely because it sprang free. Since I've never been much of the explaining or apologizing type, I simply reached out and snatched it with an acceptance that my welcome there had been overstayed.

Her brothers saw me out. They picked me up off my feet and began charging me down the hallway, like fucking barbarians readying their battering ram, my head, both yelling. When we arrived at the door Mom had opened, and the brothers began to heave me, I reached for and gripped their collars as tight as I could, clenching everything as I was tossed and it all went black.

When I came to and found myself laying in shit-smelling mud or actual shit, having crashed through the rotten wood of a front deck and into the ground below, I also found my attackers knocked fucking out. Their foreheads had met with force the uncompromising base of what was an overstated and titanic front wooden door. My vision was correcting as I was crawling out of the porch, wiping myself off when Girl came running up behind me, hysterical. She put me in the car saying, "We have to go, we have to go, fucking go!" I did. It sounded like someone was trying to shoot our tires.

The music was loud as we drove a blitz back to the city, hitting two hundred and forty kilometers an hour to "Nas Ne Dogonyat" on empty country roads because she called me soft. Girl kept dipping into the bag for bumps, and would either snort them or smear pinches into my nose or across my gums or into my ass. When I asked her if she had had enough, she went down on me for eleven kilometers. When she came up to place an obtuse pile on the tip of my cock to snort, all she kept saying, over and over, "This is going to be the best night."

I don't remember the first club from the last…there were a handful. Every room we entered, I sat back and watched her own everything inside. She was a wonder. I feared for the worlds her beauty could conquer, holding so much in the palm of one's hand. There was a sobering moment at the club that could have served as a warning to the shit that would soon find me. The owner approached at the end of the night and apologized. Something was wrong with my credit. He told me the last bottle would be compliments of the house, so I took everything that was left in my pocket and put it in his, thinking little of what he had said. It was late. Girl turned to me and said something like eight hours. In the morning, she was getting on a plane to shoot in Bermuda. It was our last night. I began to realize the possibility that in the incredibly short amount of time I had spent with Girl, she had cleaned out the one hundred and twenty-seven thousand dollars that were supposed to get me to the last fiscal quarter of 2006, and to my next financial recharge.

I stepped out of the shower and the hired muscle handed me a towel, eyes on my every move. I was actually fucked. You'd think a person of my family standing would have options in a dead end situation such as the one I was in. That's where you'd be wrong. That's where you'd underestimate the reach of my father. I had only one option. I created a small diversion and moved calmly to the dresser, where I scavenged the drawers, tossing aside all the clothes I had brought, all the designer shit Girl had bought and left behind. There it was, sitting in the bottom of the last drawer, just staring me in the face…what was left of our key. To get out of town and beyond, I was going to have to sell it.

When I'm in Prague, I like to go to this place called The Palace, which is really just a classed up way of saying brothel or prostitute congregation. As part of a healthy life regimen, I believe every man, woman, and legal child should partake in hired sex. I've never understood why the sex-worker community has since the beginning of time had to endure such scorn, when they clearly provide public service. There is no better way to learn about yourself than to pay someone to fuck you.

The Palace is like any big city apartment building – four floors, ten rooms per. You arrive at a room, discuss the terms of use with the tenant, and off you go. Most of the rooms are themed. That's to say the hooks make each their own, décor and all. When I visit Sylvia in 3-H and note the soft magenta walls, the recessed and angled lighting, the stereo with pristine surround sound, I feel the warmth she's striving to create. When we get to the bed, to her taut Egyptian sheets and effervescent mattress, sometimes I only want to lie there with her, to know her. Of course that never happens, but we do fuck a couple clicks down...gentle even, at times. Tatiana in 4-B, on the other hand, has only white walls, a stiff and bruised IKEA bed, shower, and an iPod that exclusively plays spoken-word Russian trance. She's a minimalist who means business, and has only one speed. Devil tornado.

The problem I have with The Palace, because in writing I should consider this a problem, is that I only go when I'm flying on the fringe of control. That usually means cocaine. The only problem I have with Prague, because in writing I should consider this a problem, is that everything is hyper-easy to score. When I have a lot, I do a lot. Therefore, when I'm in Prague, you'll often find me at The Palace. In fact, I'd be willing to bet I've been with everyone at least once...or at least that I'd been in every room. The turnover rate isn't as high as one might expect, but like all places, people still leave.

Jamz was my guy at The Palace. He was a full six foot, five-inch destroyer, and was working the door when I showed up. He could spin discs too, and split his time upfront or in the booth as a surprisingly capable Palace DJ. We liked each other, and had rapport. I mentioned that I only had thirty-two Euros. Jamz told me there had been a crackdown. Customers had been taking advantage of Palace credit and girls had been giving up free lays. He motioned to a newly installed door camera, made mention of management's recent and strict five-hundred Euro browsing rule. Zero exceptions he said, not even for John Durban. Everything was riding on my ability to get inside, and he either saw the desperation in my eyes or remembered all the times I had taken care of him. Whatever it was, he decided to let me in on the grounds that I did him a solid. He said exactly, "John Durban. You've got to fuck Milga in 2-J. But you can't just fuck her. For me, you gotta do it real nice."

Milga was something of a legend at The Palace. She had been there since the beginning, 1972, back when it was just an apartment building and she was just a hook trying to make ends meet, turning tricks, working from home. When management took over and the joint got an upgrade, she wouldn't leave without a fight, so they kept her on as housemother. She managed every girl, every customer, every touch in every room. Over the years, she also did so much acid, most of it bad acid, the drug permanently crossed her. Or so the story goes. Earlier in the chapter, I mentioned I'd graced every Palace room. But I'd never stepped foot in 2-J. It doesn't happen. No one steps foot in 2-J anymore.

The stairs leading to the second floor were creaking as I made my way up. So was the second floor hallway. Every room I passed brought a seller, A-I. Seven women, two men. They all stood and witnessed my march down the line, all the way down, until I stopped on 2-J and knocked. Milga's door seemed to open itself a crack and I walked in. She was already on the bed, wrapped in a dull white robe that must have at one time been gleaming. She smiled true, but with false teeth. Two were gold. One of her eyes was considerably lazy. Her hair was fried and red and shooting, ends split everywhere like a heap of steel wool. She was at least twice my age. Nonetheless, there was something captivating her performance. Beauty. Beauty in sadness. Beauty in dedication. Beauty in confidence. The door closed itself as Jamz called on the house intercom to tell her about my special request – her legendary pussy. She thanked him, then demanded he watch, then motioned me to approach, which I did while taking off my clothes in an extended striptease. Then, for the next hour or so, I did what I was told to do. I fucked her real nice.

I ran up the stairs to Natalia, 4-E, thinking she would buy the coke and break me out of Prague. She didn't, and instead took a quarter in exchange for a hookup she claimed was solid gold. There was no negotiation. She removed her cut while writing out directions and saying things like The Baron and Zlata and, "I would hurry."

The streets were empty as I approached the address on Zlata, repeating numbers in my head – one four two seven six floor six, one four two seven six floor six, one four two seven six floor six. Then I came to face it, Zlata one four two seven six. The lower level windows were boarded up and scorched. Arson, maybe. There were holes in the boards, room enough for squatters or homeless. I took a breath. All I had to do was find floor six, and some guy called The Baron. As I hit the first step, walking up, I immediately felt I should have had a gun, something to tuck into the back of my pants and hide under my jacket, insurance in case the world started to flip. I had nothing, fucking nothing and so my eyes scoured the wasteland. That's when I saw it – destiny in the form of a rusted hammer. It was just sitting there in the gutter, my Excalibur, with a light stream of brown water rushing over and around it. I picked it up, tucked it into the back of my pants and entered the building as an earless man passed me. He grunted when we bumped, this troll, and I continued, ready and willing as I climbed the stairs, one step at a time, all the way to floor six.

Rooms 6-1 to 6-7 lined the walk. I thought of how amateur it would seem for me to knock on every door. I hated amateur shit and people and things. At the end of the hall, the last door on the right was marked 6. Just 6. It had to be the place. I took a deep breath and knocked. There was a loud crash inside, then something giant and metal collapsed before someone approached the door, said something in Czech before I said English. I could feel he was looking at me through the peep for some time before the door finally creaked open and revealed half his face. He was easily the most sinister looking man I had ever seen, gangly and young and gigantic and ugly. He said, "So you're The Durban and I'm The Baron." I showed him what was left of the key and he opened the door, let me inside. Shit was everywhere and the place smelled like an abandoned rotting zoo...so rare and awful, I threw up in the sink when he momentarily left the room to put on some music. There were crates of coconut milk labeled in Russian and stacked to the ceiling. He was high as fuck on something, but I couldn't tell what it was.

INSERT SKETCH: THE BARON STANDING OVER JOHN – BIRDS HANGING – COCONUT MILK

The Baron was at least six foot six and at most one hundred and fifty pounds. His eyes caved deep into the back of his skull. There were one dozen birds stuffed and hanging from his ceiling: parakeets, toucans, crows, an eagle – tied by their ankles and dangling in the breeze. The Baron told me about them, about how he was an avid collector of birds and then, how it wasn't morbid to collect the dead, but rather the opposite. He claimed it to be an affirmation of life. I nodded and agreed with everything he said, hoping to expedite the process so I could sell my shit and get the fuck out. I thought he would chill once I was inside, once we had met and he had sized me up. He didn't, or wouldn't, or wasn't capable. He eventually told me to sit. I did. He told me to take out the drugs. I did. He took a taste and smiled. I watched as he counted out 15 quick claps of his hands before his bicep cramped and he complained of pain. Then he got up and jumped around the room until one of his calves cramped and he complained of pain. In hindsight, I'm fairly certain The Baron was harmless. But at the time, I have to say that everything he was doing, everything about that scene had removed my cool. I started thinking about where I was and what was happening…then all I could think of was *Scarface* and the Miami chainsaw ambush and watching a brother of mine get carved to pieces in front of me as his blood and insides fly all over my face and into my mouth. I didn't have a brother. It didn't matter. Feelings transfer. The Baron was pacing and yelling and escalating and he began telling this story that drifted between Czech and English when out of nowhere, shitty Russian disco came on and it was thumping the room and the water of my soul was boiling and rushing up to the edge of the pan, scalding and bubbling. He began dancing, twisting and bobbing his way to an open drawer and I became convinced in that moment The Baron was pure evil. Everything that happened next happened fast. The Baron pulled a stack of cash from the drawer. He approached until he stood before me and smiled. Then he made a move, a reach – he was reaching for the back of his pants and my mind screamed fuck he's going for the gun you're dead you're fucking dead.

There's a very distinct sound that happens when you clear out a man's teeth with a rusted hammer. Their enamel, if cared for correctly, has enough fortitude to give the metal of that hammer a slight ring, like a faint game show bell. I will never, ever forget that ring. Or the sight of The Baron curled and weeping on the floor. In his outstretched hand, he was holding a plastic figurine – a middle aged and mustached pilot in a red airplane. The Red Baron. That's what he was reaching for. That was his move. Across the plastic wings, The Baron had scribbled his contact information. Between my pity and the sounds of his wailing, I tried to compliment his unique business card, and thank him for thinking enough of me to make an attempt at staying in touch. I was touched. I tried to apologize as he was going into shock. There was a lot of blood and I threw up again, but on his couch. I called an ambulance before counting out half the money he was going to give me. Then I left the other half in a drawer next to the bag, and locked it. There were more apologies, endless apologies before I backed out of the room, out of the hall, the building, the street Zlata, and Prague.

SANTORINI
November 15, 2006

I couldn't walk correctly. That was my first thought when I stood and began to exit the ferry. After spending an entire night sleeping on a hard plastic bench and tumbling on rough Grecian waters, I came to the deck. The sun was rising around a severely pitched and slow-approaching coastline. Pus was pouring from my feet as it had been for the past fourteen hours, and the cloth of my socks was peeling then re-attaching to open wounds I had given myself the previous morning. I was dropping myself into a new place, again, and I was so desperately trying to remove the menace of pain from my face, from my raw feet so that I might in some way salvage the island's first impression of me.

Santorini was supposed to be my last stop in Europe, because I was down to my last dollars. After starting in Paris, I moved from Munich to Prague to Amsterdam to Bruges to Brussels to Dublin to London to Barcelona to Nice to Monaco to Riomaggiore to Venice to Rome to Pompeii to Athens to Santorini. I saved the last two stops to feed my fascination for Grecian history, but there was one legend in particular I had set out to live, of a messenger named Pheidippides, who after a great victory over the Persian army at the Battle of Marathon in 490 BC, was called upon to run the news to Athens, about twenty-five miles away. He made it to the Acropolis, knelt and said, "Nike! Nenikekiam!" Meaning, "Victory! Rejoice, we conquer!" Then he died.

It was cold the morning I set out to run Pheidippides' path, frigid. I remember shivering in the street, teeth chattering before I began. Three miles in, the dark skies turned noticeably darker and by mile five, the rain had come and my shoes were soaked and sloshing. I should have stopped, knowing of the pain that would later come as a result of running on wet feet for hours. By mile nine, the skin on my feet had grown soft and wrinkled and by eleven, the first layer had been lifted and torn from the heel of my foot, then another layer from the ends of my arches, then another by the pads and knuckles of my toes. By mile thirteen, I was in trouble because by seventeen, my white Nikes had run red with blood. I pressed on.

For as long as I can remember, running has been a correcting force in my life. When I was very young, I had trouble in school. Counselors told my parents I had conditions to explain the ticks in my eyes, nose, grinding teeth, incessant tapping of my fingers and toes. I used to have an uncontrollable stutter. For weeks, I'd go out in public and literally be unable to speak, afraid I'd choke on my words, afraid I'd stand out, afraid of humiliation. For a couple years, I was mistakenly diagnosed with a speculative form of Autism. My father didn't believe any of this. One day when I was still very young, my parents threw me a party at our first home, for just the four of us. There were balloons and I ate pizza and cake but it wasn't my birthday. At the end of the night, we sat down as a family and my father declared we were done letting people tell us I was unfit to thrive, or that there was anything insurmountably wrong with me. He said, "Today on, adversity will be your gift. It will become strength." He chose his words so kindly, and determinately, I cried and believed it all. Then he pulled out a new pair of the most beautiful running shoes I had ever seen and said, "Build your heart. Everything else will follow." From that next morning, three hundred mornings per year and many of them with my father, I'd wake up to an alarm and go running. Some of them hold the fondest memories of my young life.

Twenty-five miles is a great distance. I'd been going for over two hours and my feet were numb from pain, torn and bloody. At mile twenty, I thought back to walking the streets of Munich and of a girl named Jocina who rode with me on the overnight train from Paris. She was going home to see her friends and was so honest and elegant. She wanted me to kiss her that night on the train. I didn't. I couldn't. She wanted me to meet her friends in the Spaten tent at

Oktoberfest, to ride bikes in the English Garden the Sunday before I left, to show me her city, to know me, some American boy. That was all she wanted. It would have been so easy. When she called, I never picked up. At mile twenty-one, I thought of the fairytale city Prague and of how I missed Durban by only a matter of days. I wondered what might have been in store for the two of us and of my walking the streets past midnight, in the mood for a fight, trying to tempt whatever lurked. At twenty-two, I thought of the skate parks, weed, and museums in Amsterdam, and of the beer and chocolate in Bruges. Twenty-three, waking up in a Brussels train station stairwell to the fight I found with some drunk gang roughing up a homeless guy and his dog. Twenty-three still, to endless drinks and watching a genius two-piece fiddle band in Dublin's Temple Bar. Twenty-four, the Mediterranean: The Spanish Steps in Barcelona, the Promenade des Anglais in Nice, propositioning to be kept by older women trapped in the majesty of Monaco, my tossing some crazed and attacking farmer's goat off a mini-cliff while lost in Italy's Cinque Terra. Twenty-five, Venice and Rome, walking the lips of Vesuvius and trying to beg out eruption. I reached Athens. The rain had stopped. I didn't want to take off my shoes, didn't want to face what was underneath so I took a cab to my hotel, grabbed my bag, paid my dues and jumped a ferry to what was said to be one of the emptiest islands in all of Greece.

There's one grueling road that runs from the Port of Santorini to the island's largest town, Fira. To get to Fira or beyond, you have to negotiate a place to stay from one of the travel offices lining the port walk. There is no walking. There was a girl named Sophie in one of the offices. I told her I needed a place to stay. She said, "What were you waiting for do you know what it feels like to walk up that road when everyone leaves you behind?" She said everything in near perfect English, called me a fool American, and told me there were rooms in both Fira and Oia. There was coldness about her as she began on a disenchanted rant about sunsets in Oia being the best in the world. I could see that maybe she was once upon a time the exact person who believed in such things, and I began to wonder if I believed in such things anymore. I used to. She said I needed to settle on Fira or Oia, so that I could fall into company during what was considered to her, the cold season. I told her I was looking for something else, something less popular. She rolled her eyes, "Perissa it is."

We drove across the rocky guts of Santorini. There was nothing there, just dust, dirt, mountain. Sophie said that in the summers, you don't notice the land between, that there's too much happening, too many people around, "All it is — fun, fun, fun." When she asked why I was hobbling, I told her. She laughed and shook her head.

We pulled up to this place on the water called Villa Holiday Beach. She took me inside, stepped behind the front desk, had me sign a few papers and gave me a room. She said it would be fifteen Euros per day. When I told her I was taking the ferry back in the morning, she got pissed at the brevity of my stay and said, "Well I won't be here to take you back." She showed me where to leave the key and cash when I checked out. I was being abandoned on the honor system. When I thanked her, and I'm not sure what for, she stepped in and kissed me on each cheek. Then she got in her car and took off.

I walked into my room and closed the door; saw the posted room rates that fetched as much as two hundred Euros in peak season. Inside, it was nice and clean. The sheets were pressed and folded. I placed my things on the floor and fell onto the bed. I thought back to all of the alleys and trains and concrete floors I had been sleeping in and on over the past couple months, and was asleep in seconds.

I woke up starving and the clock said half past eight. From my hotel, I walked a half-mile down the road to the closest and only set of potential shops where I might actually buy something to eat. There were a couple boarded gift shops, an abandoned rental office and then a tailor shop or bakery that had pressed shirts on one wall and breads on the other. It was black inside save a flicker of light coming from the back room. A television was on. I knocked, then waited. Then I knocked again and harder, then waited. For the next ten minutes, I kept knocking. An older woman's face appeared above the door. She stood there and settled into a good stare, this drained look in her eye. I reached into my pocket and pulled a stash of Euros. She let me inside.

I bought some of everything she had: cookies, raisin bread, pizza bread, pretzel bread, muffins, a sausage croissant, two apple cakes, and Milko. Her name was Zelda. She sewed a hole in my pants free of charge, and pointed me to the famed Perissa black sand beach, saying, "But empty bad storm is come."

The main stretch of restaurants and bars that line the beach side of Perissa were closed for the season. Human silence filled the world. Waves trickled before me, cracking and moving against the black sand, which would shine under sparse stars and moonlight. I finished everything in Zelda's bag. It was maybe the most satisfying meal I had ever eaten.

The dark sky above me seemed impossibly lit in a shade of pink. I studied it and sat for an hour before lightning broke stillness to reveal a marshmallow and rushing sky. Thunder followed, shaking my new world to its bones. I could feel surges move through the pads in my shoes, into the blisters and torn wounds on my feet. The rains came. Drizzle turned to the pour of a vicious island storm. I got up and began to walk again, watching as I moved, more lightning cutting reveals into the jagged and abandoned land. It seemed only moments had passed and the rain had drenched my body. Drops of water formed on my brow, would drip as I'd blink, as I fought to see far enough ahead to merely place one foot in front of the next, to stay on path. I hadn't yet turned back, having unknown intention of returning to my room at Villa Holiday Beach.

At the end of the Perissa beaches, there's a road that veers left between two hills and eventually leads to Sophie's famed Oia. Between strobes of the sky, the passageway looked mythological, as if braving that road, that night could have transported me anywhere, across Earth or into a dream. I walked the road to its peak, looked down and onto the land ahead of and behind me. Then I stopped, stood, watched an escalating symphony of storm. It was growing still, maybe forever. I began to urge her on, begging through telepathic satellites in my mind, hand raised into the air. Show me your might. Land and charge through me. With every flash denied, a shiver followed. I was certain that something, somewhere was hearing my every wish.

INSERT SKETCH: RAIN AND LIGHTNING – BURN'S FIST IN THE AIR – DOGS CIRCLING

Halfway home, the rains stopped. The clouds cleared and the moon cast its full light. I felt alone and didn't want to be, not anymore. Out the corner of my eye, a white blur sped past my legs and slowed into a trot twenty feet ahead of me. It was a starved white Labrador dog, mirroring my pace. More motion shot about my flanks. A Doberman ran out from underneath the trench of a bus stop, dropped into a trot five feet behind me. From inside an abandoned house, two dark terriers appeared across the house lot and dashed into formation by my sides. I took a picture. On quiet and dark Santorini, my flash must have stretched for miles. Maybe other dogs saw it as a beacon. Maybe they just lived along the road and mine was the best show in town. Whatever reason they had to be there, our numbers grew from five to seven to nine to eleven. When I stopped to fix my shoes or to give my feet a break from walking, The Dogs of Santorini would peel off the road to patrol in excited circles or figure eights. The moment of my return, they'd fall back into formation. I put on my iPod. Playing "Kashmir," I raised its tiny headphones towards the sky, full of rare desire to let the world witness me, the troop, everything then.

Up ahead, I could see the small and fiery glow of a cigarette being smoked. It was Zelda, standing outside her combo shop. She winked when I showed up, then kissed me twice when I left, because I had bought everything left in her store that could be eaten. The dogs and I walked a quarter-mile from Zelda, a quarter-mile from my hotel before I carefully emptied the food onto a dry patch by the side of the road. I watched the dogs eat, thanked them for their service, and left them behind.

At the back end of the corridor, by the pool at Villa Holiday Beach, I could see orange light flickering against the clay-paneled roof. I turned the corner to find Sophie, harsh Sophie sitting alone next to a burning fire. She said, "Fira is a drag. I never come to Perissa because I don't want to be alone. But now you're here." She asked if I was crazy. I answered no. She asked where I'd been. I didn't have a good answer. She used the word gallivanting. I thought that was precious. She didn't understand.

I hadn't paid Sophie enough attention when we first met. She was too much. I had come to Santorini to be alone, maybe to pay some inaudible homage to Michael, but with her there, I felt a shift inside. I didn't want to feel what I'd been feeling anymore. I said a lot of things, and she just listened. Not many people are capable of that. She told me I was the reason she came to Perissa. We stayed outside until the horizon started to glow, until the air grew too cold to endure, until we had no wood left to burn. When silence fell, I kissed her. We went inside and slept for a couple hours before the alarm rang out and she drove me back to port.

BERLIN
December 25, 2006

We were on a night train and Durban shook me awake. He handed me a bitter glass of juice and said, "Keep it moving." I'd been asleep for a short stretch before he was inches from my face and insistent. I drank what he gave me and almost threw up. When I didn't, everything felt better.

When he called me last week, I was washing dishes in a country kitchen outside of Venice. I told him what I was doing, and he said he could get me a better job, something I could do on the road, and to not worry about money. He told me to trust him, which I didn't really. But I did leave the job in Venice, agreeing to meet him in Copenhagen for a couple moderately behaved nights before he chipped away and chipped away until things spun out of control. I wasn't ready to go home to the States, someone couldn't easily leave or deny John Durban, and it was Christmas. So I was in for Berlin.

We took a cab to get fit with two last-minute tuxedos from the finest tailor in town. Burn wanted to know more about where we were going and what we were doing, but realized at some point I was offering nothing and had nothing more to say about it. It would all be revealed. Or, it wouldn't. Once we were fit and dressed, we began driving to a compound on the outskirts of Mitte. Judging by past events I had attended with the organizers, I knew Burn would be presented with something unique, and that I wouldn't be bored. Germans are fucked. Or, being in Germany fucks people. That's always been my experience.

I kept asking where we were going and Durban kept repeating, "The funhouse," and, "Stop talking." We eventually arrived at a dark, gothic building that stood out starkly amongst uniformed streets and militant architecture. Beneath the glow of night, the building appeared haunted. At first, I didn't want to go inside. I didn't want to know of or be a part of whatever existed behind those doors. Durban gave his name to a line of armed guards before a young and beautiful girl no older than sixteen escorted us inside. A fire roared in the center courtyard. It felt mismanaged and on the verge of chaos. The heat was enormous. On the inside of the building, an exposed ramp slowly wove its way up the four stories and towards the open sky. The young girl looked back at us and said, "This way, dinner is served." She was very practiced and inhuman. When we arrived at the dining room, two seats were left open on the right side of a table shaped like a crucifix. There must have been forty people around the table, all suddenly quiet with odd eyes on us. Durban took every step of our disrupting arrival in stride. Once we moved to our seats and sat, conversations began again. I don't know what anyone was talking about or why Durban had spent even a moment calling these people his friends. It didn't seem like he knew any of them at all. There were no introductions or inclusions. At some point early on, Durban was staring at someone sitting on the far end of the table. It was a well-kept, handsome man. He was about our age and wouldn't take his eyes off Durban. And Durban wasn't flinching. He said, "You remember that story I told you about the mafia princess I knocked up in Moscow? That's her brother, the prince." A waiter arrived and set Champagne in front of us. Then everyone raised their glasses and drank to nothing. Giant beds were delivered to the four corners beside the table. Thirty-two naked bodies followed of incongruent men and women. Within minutes and by the time the first course was delivered, some of them began fucking. Soon, others joined. At that moment, I was somehow starving, staring at a rare and bloody piece of meat on my plate. There were no utensils so I picked up the meat with my bare hands and put it in my mouth, chewing as a cacophony of coital moans began to fill the room.

I was staring and wondering aloud why they hadn't hired more attractive, less regular people. Only three of

them were even good at what they were doing. The production just felt lazy, until I realized the priceless and loaded acts unfolding. Money is a hell of a thing. What the organizers had likely done, because it's what I would have done, was hire people to conduct interviews based on some false pretense to find couples both in love and in need. Offers would be made. Selected couples would be given a night to build rationalizations before eventually coming to agreements, or not. The treatment of those electing to proceed would appear delicate and respectful throughout the delivery of services, right up until the point of performance. Then behind the final curtain as the couples would be gathering their bravery and probably an unexpected feral excitement for imminent things to come, scores of other nude and prepped and delicately treated couples would also converge. Organizers would divide the collective into four groups in their biting German tongues, away from their lovers. My guess is they lost a pair, but no more than two, as the screening process would have already deemed them all suffocated enough to not abandon course.

Once the couples were divided, and began to understand what was happening, the room became enveloped by such exquisite tension, even I felt the potential of it devouring us all. Those seated that didn't understand quickly began to, as the hired and mismatched bodies began to absorb each other in a torrent of brutal desire. At first, the most noticeable thing was sadness or jealousy. There were also several obvious catalysts in the group who had no allegiances, and were only placed there to ensure things got started quickly. There was one outburst where a pained man tried to cross the table to stop another man from entering his husband. He was quickly quelled and removed. Anger or remorse built into retribution as several in the group started to cum and sounds of anguish rose through the room. Still, eventually, most seemed to finish. Some went twice. There must have been incentive clauses within the agreement that only true emotional stoics could enact. Those that didn't perform were threatened harshly, either through withheld payment or veiled physical harm. At least that's how I would have handled it.

Once the show had ended, bodies were ushered off and props were removed. It was like nothing ever happened. Everyone moved on and courses of food and drink kept showing up. Durban looked at me and then around the room and said plainly, "I am not entertained." Someone from across the table made a claim to know John and tried to start a conversation he wouldn't acknowledge. He was growing impatient, and upset, and began to talk out loud, making a scene when the deranged looking Russian prince named Alexandr stood and commanded the room with, "John Durban!" Then, "Why don't you tell us who is your friend?" There was a rage in his eyes and in his voice.

I watched Burn watch Alexandr, the two of them in standoff. Burn's gaze grew quickly vicious. There was reason why Alexandr was never permitted any position of real relevance inside of his family's syndicate. He gave the appearance of weakness, nervous and graceless, with pitiful command of the room, and of himself, and of his emotions. These attributes had everything to do with his sexuality wishing to exist authentically in a country and organization that would never allow it. His oldest sister was a reckoning woman, and was chosen over him to carry the family name as he was shuffled aside. His youngest sister was the source of his great discontent towards me, and so it seemed that discontent was being transferred onto Burn. Also, he was in love with me. I was bored and careless so I told him and the room that Burn was a fatalist to dying young, and that because of it, he was the great love of

my life. When I was done speaking, I pulled Burn close to me. Then I kissed him.

Alexandr seemed hurt and tortured and stifled by what Durban had said and done. He began, "If this is true, and you believe the fickle path to life is so certain, then I have a story you both must hear." I'll paraphrase his story for clarity, because he didn't tell it well. Also, because that night changed everything. A long time ago, his great uncle Orlov was second in command to the boss of Moscow. Orlov had a wife he loved and an identical twin brother who also served as his greatest confidant. One summer night, there was a bombing at a club that supposedly killed Orlov. But he wasn't in the blast. Instead, a rival kidnapped and held him. In the months that passed during his captivity, Orlov's brother and wife grieved his death together, then fell in love. Then the brother became second in command to the boss of Moscow. Everyone moved on. Some days for food, the captors would throw live rats into Orlov's cell, which he would have to catch and eat raw if he wanted to survive. Alexandr credited the thought of a loving wife as what kept Orlov alive, until the day his captors drove him to the center of Red Square on Christmas Eve and threw him out of a moving car. He was famished and near dead, freezing and delirious, and essentially began dragging himself in the direction of his home and family. The captors had cut off an arm at the elbow and one of his ears was lost to gangrene. His right eye was gouged and infected. Broken bones never healed. He arrived home and was greeted by his former guards with disbelief. Then he saw his wife in his brother's arms. Alexandr claimed that night was the only time Orlov ever shed a tear, "Which fell to the ground with the last shreds of his iron will." That last part, he told well.

The captors turned out to be small time thugs, anarchists with intention of starting a war – to watch Orlov take the city apart piece by piece searching for retribution. Instead, the only retribution he would seek was on his dearest wife, and brother. That's when Alexandr said something in

Russian that made Russian speaking guests laugh before he said in English, "That day, with great sorrow, the Orlov was born." Orlov called a trusted aide and ordered his wife and brother to be killed. The order was to be buried deep within the family's network, designed untraceable and without recourse, even for Orlov. But then he compromised, rolled a single dice, which landed on four. He told his wife and brother to leave, which they did. Four years later, on a remote island at the edge of the world in Sri Lanka, they were found together, and were killed.

Alexandr was more than a little pissed. I knew it previously, when he could have accidentally had me dropped on my head from a great height in Moscow. And I knew it that night, when we first walked into the room and I caught him leering. I had physically and emotionally harmed and discarded his sister, and that was a serious offense. So, in no way should I have also used Burn to tempt Alexandr's rage, but I did. Burn went fucking off in response. He took the story as a threat to our safety. Or, maybe our honor. It didn't matter. Nothing mattered as Burn foamed and screamed, first at Alex and then the entire room, about their hollow souls and eyes and hearts. For the first time ever, I was trying to keep things from escalating further, to bury and shine with charm, all the wild threats Burn was making. He was detached and wild. I had fed him far too much and he had not slept. He wasn't right in the head. The room had quickly turned on us when Alexandr said, "I have not questioned your honor. You are the one questioning it now." Burn made a move to get to Alex when his personal security appeared and stepped between them. Alex said, "There is no need. No need." Alex picked up his phone and dialed a number. He asked to be connected to someone, and waited. As he was waiting, he said, "When I give you the phone, all you have to do is say your name. If you are both what you say you are. If you believe what you

say you believe." Burn stared until Alex lowered the phone from his ear and then slid it across the table. Burn caught it. He looked to me then. I shook my head, instruction to preserve our dignity while conveying the existence of bad people in the world. I was also trying to provide Burn that this was not likely some party stunt, but he was too far gone. I reached out to stop him when he lifted the phone and stated his name. The crowd gasped, and I froze. The room went silent. Even Alexandr appeared shocked. The line was still open on the table. In that moment, I did the only thing I could. I leaned over the phone, stated my own name, and ended the call. Alexandr's voice shook with a quiver as he said, "It's settled then. Now you are truly fatalist, compliments of myself and my great Uncle Orlov. Enjoy the rest of your time together." Alexandr and his contingent walked out.

There was a car waiting for us out front. It was bulletproof. We didn't know where we were going. Durban told the driver, "Maybe a long tour." He was sitting across from me with his hands on his knees and was looking through the tinted windows. He appeared in a trance. I told him I was sorry. He didn't say anything, so I told him again. He just said, "That's alright, Burn. That's alright." Then he looked up to the moon roof inside of the car, opened it and stood. I stood to meet him. The world outside slid past us. Durban put his arm around me as a light rain fell. Millions of tiny daggers against our skin.

Durban got me a job as a travel writer for one of the big magazines back in the states. I'm getting paid to write briefs on the places we go, from days in Stellenbosch and Simonstown to our forever nights on Long Street. If my appointment sounds like nepotism and a scam, it is. Durban knows people everywhere. And people everywhere are either willing to do things for him or are willing to follow his instructions. Even though I had reservations about taking the job for all these reasons, I did ultimately accept. The work I do is passable. People are fine with it.

I recently spent a few days in Kenya after following Durban down a violent spiral of new cities across Europe and Northern Africa, eventually waking up on a hospital bed in Mombasa. The doctor gave me fluids and antibiotics, and then also brought in a counselor to have a sincere talk with me about what could happen if I kept things up. Durban waited outside during the talk. After the doctor and counselor spoke with me, they moved into the hallway to update Durban, my apparent intervening friend. I watched closely through the glass viewing window as a great many horrific things were revealed. Durban raised his hands to cover his mouth, as if barely able to handle the thought of it all. He acted faint and shook his head in disgust, then looked back at me with such disappointment, the counselor actually reached out to comfort him. She shook her head and stroked his arm. Everything was a game to him.

When we first showed up in Cape Town, Durban punched a code to a house owned by people he called, "The Patricks." Once inside, he walked to a safe behind a foyer painting, punched another code and opened the door to millions in Rand. His whole body seemed weak and wavering from exhaustion before he led me into the kitchen and pointed me towards a steel cabinet. He said, "Anything you'll need is in there." Then he shuffled off to the closest bedroom and slept for the next 5 days. When I opened the cabinet, there were rows of pill vials and several powders, all meticulously labeled and at our disposal. There were times in the middle of those first few nights, where I would wake up to the sounds of Durban in agony. He'd shuffle to the cabinet and take something to feed a craving or to calm things down before heading back to bed or out for a drive. We didn't see much of each other those first few days.

The house was a vision. It sat high in the mountains beneath the Twelve Apostles – South Africa's postcard and backyard mountain range that stretches the country's southern coastline. Most days, a thick white mass of cloud appears over the top of Table Mountain, the king of twelve. I'd sit out back, alone, watching the cloud pour off the mountains and vanish. A beautiful, admirable disappearing act.

The compromise that Durban and I began to make in Cape Town was that there would be actual sleep at the end of nights. That way, every morning, we would have to return to ourselves, and face the things we had done. Durban despised this. I saw great value in it. Every morning, like I used to do as a boy, I'd get up and go running down the winding coastline of Victoria Drive. On and on. On the way back, close to town and the Pick n' Pay, there's a small beach just below the Houghton Steps. It's always empty. After every run, after all my fight had been left behind, I'd take a concealed path down to the ocean, and ease my way into the freezing South African Atlantic. The cold would seep over me and crawl through my skin, until I was floating and clean.

One day Burn said I was clearly a nymphomaniac. I said he clearly was not. The only reason we were even discussing my sexual behavior was because I had asked him to limit my suitors so that I might move towards some path of perceived sexual normalcy, if for no other reason than to test will and the depth of his assessment. I should also make clear that our discussion had less to

do with the girls I would pick up and was more designed to dull my appetite for high-end prostitution, which Burn claimed was both addiction feeding and diluting my capacity for genuine emotion. Even after what we have been through, he still believes in irrational things, like perseverance and betterment. When I assure him we don't need to know love to know love, he placates and agrees. When I tell him he needs to fuck as much as I need to fuck less, he becomes disconnected and perturbed, saying things like I'm not you. Often, if not always, I feel like he's picking battles with me, and that our ramping discussions are only precursor to a never ending battle between two people who are both so alike and not. But I don't mind. When it comes to genuine matters of the heart, he's the boss. I believe there is much to be learned. He loved his brother deeply and then lost him in such a way. I also started to believe he had loved a great many things in his life before stopping altogether. A shift like that creates echoes that will always remain. So when I can, I pull him, pry him, study anything and everything he'll give in an attempt to form a better understanding of him. Often, he doesn't even need to speak and it feels like I'm being condescended. But that's okay. I'm good. He mostly has the right.

John was going through something. He had been making at least somewhat of an effort to not always black out and take me with him. We were moving toward something bigger, and talked about it often during our time on the Cape. We had both been good, feeding off the land, food and sights, actual nourishment at times, culture over whatever vacant and deranged things Durban would have otherwise been lining up. I think new patterns were the biggest challenge for him. Though he had seen most of the world, I'm not sure how much of it he had actually seen.

We were six weeks into our stay when Durban got a call from the Patricks. They were finally coming down from

Johannesburg. One of the things I've gathered about Durban, life, and the general way of the world is that the phenomenon of unstoppable force does exist. Pertaining to me, it existed in the form of John Durban. I knew that if he tried to curb himself too quickly, he would never survive, and would likely bring me down with him. So even though I knew the Patricks were likely to make things complicated again, I also understood maybe they needed to happen. Durban told me their move was to buy out the Dunleen's pool and most of the hotel so they could put on the best weekend party in town. Eventually one morning, they pulled up to the house around eleven, driving a Carrera GT and a Koenigsegg CCX, silver and black, respectively. They had the cars shipped down and evidently capped off disjointed nights by racing the winding coastline with stars in their eyes, clinging to absurd life. Of course when I saw them, I knew they were more Durban's style than mine. They pulled into the driveway and bounced out of each car, both with a girl in tow, depraved smiles on their faces. They looked like brothers but weren't, one skinny one fat, and had a presence in the neighborhood of Durban's – bred from a lifetime of wealth and privilege. Patrick was wearing a jean jacket with torn sleeves and leather because he was coming from an overnight costume party dressed as Billy Idol. Other Patric was wearing tuxedo pants with no shirt or shoes. They had gotten in the night before. Durban realized this as he was pretending to fuck the open gas tank of the Porsche. Reports ensued of a wild night and Durban became increasingly upset that he missed it.

When we got inside, Patrick dropped a case of '95 Dom Rose on the table and immediately began popping bottles with a toast about returning to the land that invented beautiful women, good friends and golden sunsets. Then he said they had just closed the biggest deal of their lives. The other Patric extended it, "Epic bru, ya have no idea."

We raced past the Clifton beaches, literally, through Bantry Bay and Sea Point, going 160 kilometers an hour

on tiny and winding roads, dodging pedestrian surfers and families, dames crammed in the back of the Porsche and scream singing "Fame" the whole way. Not Bowie. When we settled into straighter roads, Patrick opened the glove compartment and pulled a bag of green pills. He said they were harder than Ecstasy and that I'd never had anything exactly like them. Since me and Burn had something of a deal that all deals were off when the Patricks came to town, I took six of his suggested two. When we arrived at the Dunleen, there was already a line wrapping the valet lot and stretching into the street. Like I already said or should have if I haven't, everyone knows when the Patricks come to town. I scanned the waiting as we passed and was truly impressed, am always impressed with the Cape's cyclical and high-grade foreign and local talent. Like most modeling towns, girls come from all over the world to work. Though, this town is a little different. Adventure calls and raw beauty abounds. Since living well isn't as cheap as one might think, and because it's common for beautiful people to lose focus in such a wondrous world, a great number of them get caught up in doing things they should not be doing. Little good comes from starting a relationship with John Durban. They just don't know.

Durban moved out of the car ahead of us. It was obvious he had taken something affecting. I didn't care about that, or that I was watching him dance and glide across the courtyard. Dizzy, he stopped, composed himself and moved through the line waiting to get in, going to work on several girls he was planning on for later. We are all given talents, some more than others. Durban wasn't charming, he was charm – the definition, the adage – to fuck him, to be him. That day something came over me. I couldn't watch him do what he always did, wave goodbye, or do the same to myself. The next morning, I was driving to Boulders Beach to do a magazine story and to swim with penguins at the southern tip of Africa. That felt like enough. When I hinted any of these feelings to Durban, he laughed behind panic and always said the same thing, "You don't mean that…don't talk like that." Fat Patrick approached me with his bag of green pills and I was hesitant. He insisted, saying, "Come on Sammy, team effort here." He grew distrusting of me when I hesitated again. That's the kind of guy Patrick was. He took a small handful from out of the bag and stuffed them into my back pocket. Then he smiled and slapped my cheek before we walked in together, past the crowd and through a covered side entrance. The party was already at capacity. When we stepped in, a hesitant then jolting cheer bubbled up from the crowd. Inside, the Patricks had hired and flown in two DJ's, one from Beirut and the other from Dubai. I heard someone earnestly say they were ranked #3 and #11 in the world. In another corner, there was a small jazz quartet: piano, sax, bass and harmonica. These guys were locals, black as night, deep and cold like their ocean. Somehow, all three entities were finding sync, and they were good. The band was doing Miles Davis and the DJ's were taking "Billy Jean" into "Kids" with enough skill to make me want to change course and re-align with Durban. I reached into my pocket, pulled out and considered the pills…

Three days before the Patricks arrived, and delivered us to their party, my car broke down off Chapman's Peak Drive. Durban was unreachable back in Camps Bay so I was on my own. When I got towed to a mechanic in Bantry Bay, he told me to give him two hours and suggested a place he knew where I could, "Go for a sundowner and have a relax, man." He called a cab that took me a long way from town, into the mountains, up to an abandoned bar. There was a sign outside, hanging from an exterior someone had recently driven into. I stepped inside and moved across a rotting wooden floor, which felt anything but secure before I looked up to find myself standing thousands of feet in the air, before a world of endless cloud, blue sea, massive rock and plush green. I took a breath. The air tasted untouched. The cab had been winding at a grade so quickly and for so long, I lost track of how far we had climbed. The bar was empty save one girl, sitting on a stool, leaning against the wall, drinking a Castle. Her name was Michelle. She was a young brunette with tied hair, tired green eyes and a transparent tattoo that ran the length of her inside right forearm. She was from San Diego, a California girl in town to study marine research at the University Cape Town. When I sat down beside her, she had a smile that came easier than anyone's I could remember. It pulled me to her. I focused on it, obsessed. I told her I had lost what she had somewhere. She asked what. I said ease. I don't know why I offered so much so fast. I had no hesitation. She blushed. It was all probably too much. The only thing I was thinking was stay forever.

She was at the bar because her VW Beetle had broken down and the same mechanic sent her up to, "Go for a sundowner and have a relax, man." He owned the bar. We had a laugh about that. Hours passed until locals began to appear and we feared the mechanic would close us out of his shop. We shared the same cab back into town, and agreed to meet again but without a plan. Then, we split up. She was all I thought of the entire ride home, then every waking moment after. To say I liked her would be too failing. The girl stole time.

Three days later and still considering my next move at The Dunleen, Michelle was standing in front of me, appearing again. My heart leapt and threw the pills from my hand into the pool. Circling fiends dove in after them as a disappointed shake of her head nearly broke me. When she leaned over to say she was leaving but wanted to say hello first, I asked where she was going. She thought about her response before saying, "Just a drive." Then she considered things for a moment before offering me a timid invite. My eyes moved across the pool deck and stopped on Durban. He was between the DJ's, riding on top of an ice sculpture shaped like a stallion and howling at the sun. I was gone from the best party in the world in less than ten minutes.

The pills were quick. Maybe the quickest ever. Maybe I had taken too many. Of course, I wasn't thinking any of those things at the time. All I remember was seeing the music. I was trying to reach out and grab it with my hands, to eat it, to praise it. Skinny Patric would later relay. I also remember several occasions where someone affiliated with the Dunleen would approach me and attempt to escort me off grounds on grounds of what must have appeared absurdist behavior. Someone always intervened. After the initial shock of high began to level off and I was able to navigate the party with grace, my needs began to arrive. At a certain moment of the day, I remember feeling a personal clarity in seeing dozens of capable beauties getting crushed by cocktails and the sun. It was then I could not endure even another moment without tight, hot skin against mine. That's when I saw her, best in show.

I was driving Michelle's '74 VW Beetle down the stretches of Chapman's Peak Drive – a road that connects the southern parts of Cape Town to the southern parts of continent Africa. It's also arguably the most scenic road on the planet – rolling and rocky coastlines and shores so daunting I could explain them forever and not approach appropriate truth. Michelle and I hardly spoke as the wind whipped through the car. It was too loud, too hard to put anything into words. Every now and then, I'd watch her as she looked off into the ocean, hair flying and free. I wanted her in every way, every minute we spent together. She could see that in me, and so told the story of her waiting American fiancé. Hearing that, my intentions changed. We evolved quickly. I only wanted to know her, to collect everything I could in the short time we might spend together, and allow that to be enough. I'd simply seen too much to try and be anything else. In every moment we existed together, there seemed to exist a plethora of unspoken understanding.

There's a grotto at The Dunleen that I'm partial to and not many people know about. I told my new friend about it to get her in the pool, hyped it more to get her to swim beneath the pool's waterfall, under a mount of faux boulders and into what turned out to be more of a maintenance room than anything resembling my descriptions of a grotto. Clearly I hadn't been fully aware of myself the last time I took someone there. Nevertheless, I had her alone in a cave, away from the party, and her eyes were making demands of me. When all you have to do is pull a string and have them ready, things begin quickly.

It didn't take long for her to cum. And it wasn't me. She was something else. I can say that I'm well equipped as a lover. Fine. But I'm also conveniently selfless in this regard – unless she gets off fully, I am incapable, as if my doing so alone would give her and the collective a power I simply can't release. She was gripping me deeply, above the water, and I was propping her hips, holding her up with my hands, biceps and arms burning and shaking as I drove through her. She did the thing where her head fell back and her breath stopped before she clamped from the inside, before releasing softly and in melody. It was incredible to hear her song, to see her unfold the way she did, and in the state I was in. It's never tired. She fell into stillness, looked to me and kissed me before leaning back, falling onto the cement and saying exactly and so beautifully, "Fuck me again, sweet Johnny." I tried to keep up as she came three times, allowing me to witness her greatness again, then again, then again. At some point, she looked to me and asked if I was ready, asked if she could do anything to give back what I'd given. I said no and that I was perfect. I didn't want to lose what we had. She kissed me when I stopped, held me, and told me her name. Anna. She made me feel like

a kind and present lover poet. I held onto that, and to her.

Boulders Beach was emptier than it should have been. We dropped our towel and sat beside a colony of penguins. They were bullets in the water, stains of dirt sprawled on rocks in the sun, black and white soldiers marching awkwardly across the sand. We had bought a small cooler from a Pick n' Pay down the road, a six pack of Castle and a couple of African sandwiches. The sun was warm. The breeze was light. We talked about the lives we had, about the lives we were hoping to have, the lives we were supposed to be having. I didn't tell her everything. When silence fell, we sat back in the sand, taking turns falling asleep. At some point as the sun was beginning to burn out, Michelle looked to me and asked if I thought it was possible that we were presently in the moment of our lives – the one we would always look back on and measure ourselves against. I thought about it long enough that she grew impatient and asked again, as if the possibility of it was unraveling something in her, in some way – that she was spending it with me. I told her I didn't have an answer, that I wasn't capable of having an answer or that I couldn't allow myself to think in those terms anymore. I'm not sure if I made her sad or confused but she looked reflective for a moment, staring out into the ocean, maybe missing him, maybe not. Her look reminded me exactly of what I've been feeling since Durban and I left Berlin. There's a clock out there and it's always moving. The only job it has is to tick away.

We left our stuff behind and walked along the rocks until there was nowhere left to go. She took my hand and looked into my eyes. They were likely tired, and probably still a bit ravaged. She said something I'll never forget, motioning my eyes and the inside of my head, quiet, delicate, "This isn't you. Treating yourself like this. It bothers me." She turned to the ocean, still holding my hand. Then she counted to three and we leapt. I felt the plunge cover my body in a rush of cold, and held myself under the water to draw out its power, still holding her hand, feeling everything. When I came up to the surface, her face was inches from mine and covered in fading sunlight. I had never wanted to kiss someone so much. I had never wanted to just remain with someone so much.

There's a door that unlocks from the inside of the grotto, drops whomever exits back into the thick of soiree. I followed her out. She was holding my hand, guiding me. When we came into the light, I felt her hand tighten then release. The guy played for the Springboks, South Africa's pro rugby team. I saw his eyes for a moment before he charged me, lifted me off my feet and slammed me into the ground. Witnesses said my head hit a pile of clothes and shoes and otherwise would have split open onto the pool deck. Instead, I settled on leaving simple skin on the ground as our bodies came to a dragging stop. I was coming down somewhat before the incident, and returned fully as he held my neck with a hand and began smashing my face with his other fist and head and forearm. Twice, I remember seeing a spiral of grey butterflies and tasting acid in my mouth before I turned over, trying to avoid a knockout. When I did turn, there was a yank on my scalp before my forehead was repeatedly driven into stone. The next thing I remember, he was off of me and I was turning over and sitting up, watching three of The Dunleen's toughest bouncers in a literal war to restrain this guy, this howling and wild and slobbering animal. I felt warmth covering my face and didn't need to see the damage to know it was there. Anna approached with a look of concern, part mine and part hers. She apologized. I told her she was worth it.

I refused medical attention and sat down on a chair in the sun. I let one of the bottle girls prop ice across my beaten face. All I could feel was pain running through my body. At some point, the Patricks came by, tried handing me pills they claimed would take me away.

Something surprising happened. I refused. I wanted to feel it all. That's what I said to them. Then I wanted to get out of there. Where was Burn? I hadn't seen him in hours. I threw the ice off my face, stood on a table and began screaming his name. The music was so loud and everyone was so fucked that I made no impression. When my voice became too hoarse to scream and my sight began to blur and spin, the music finally stopped. Suddenly this guy, who introduced himself as Archangel Gabriel was standing in front of the band, in front of the microphone asking everyone to be quiet. He spoke of knowing the Patricks for many years, and of how he'd been following their exploits with great interest from a desk at the Joburg Star – a print journalist and, "Tireless advocate for peace." Those last four words came out like a cannon firing. They readied me. I watched the Patricks step out of the Dunleen lobby. They saw him and took off, charging the stage, out for blood, plowing through the crowd, screaming, "Shut him the fuck down!" Gabriel raised his glass into the air and said, "A toast to the Patricks...whose generosity and wealth today and forevermore are brought to you by dealing arms and lives across the destruction of Africa!" The Patricks were still racing, roaring as he closed, "Celebrate! Drink! Dance! You all contribute to this great continent's destruction!" When the Patricks made it to the base of the stage, Gabriel reached into his pocket, pulled a gun, pointed at them, and fired six shots. There was screaming and trampling and as I fought my way to the stage and saw security overtake Gabriel, I also saw the Patricks not far behind, in a rush to reveal the bullets as blanks, to rescue their party, to bury what we all knew was truth but did our best to conveniently ignore.

Michelle dropped me off in front of The Dunleen and we made no agreements about seeing each other again. Somehow, that was enough. It had to be. She had already driven away. The party was emptying. I walked through the front door and saw Durban sitting on a lounge chair. The closer I got, the more was revealed. Someone had beaten him terribly. His lip was split and he was covered in dried blood, with swollen eyes. A current ripped through me. It was good I didn't see it happen. John's a fucking fool, I know. I want to make it clear that I'm not fool enough to ignore everything, but at that point, he also belonged to me. If I had been there, if I had seen someone harm him the way they did, no matter, they would have had to kill me to stop me from returning equal harm. That's what I was thinking as I approached him.

He didn't say a word. He only stood and walked past me, as if he were trying to display a form of spite for my absence, for my not asking permission of a senselessly drugged motherfucker to leave with a girl I was so drawn to, the feeling crushed me, to lay eyes on parts of the world so big they would be sewn into me. At first, as I followed him through the lobby, I thought he wanted an apology. But he didn't. There was a mission in his step. I followed him to the front desk and watched as he was given a set of keys, as he signed his name on a series of forms. He turned, flipped me the keys and said something serene, "Hello Burn you're driving…we have to get to the house right away." Then he walked outside. I turned to the desk girl to ask what happened and she told me very bluntly that Durban took the new bride of a Springbok into the maintenance closet. She was also saying something about the Patricks when Durban's voice broke between us, calling my name from the front of the hotel, adding please at the end of his interjection, enough to know that it was a lot for me to forego questions. But I did. Maybe because he said please. For him, I knew that was a lot.

We pulled up to the Patricks' house and he told me to wait in the car. It didn't take long. He came out with a brown leather backpack and announced we were going to Langa. I took a breath and drove.

Burn was quiet the entire way. He knew where we were going, probably even knew what I had in mind. That didn't matter. Here's the thing about Burn that I most admire, besides everything…is that he reveres silence more than anyone I've ever known, more than anyone I will ever know. I'm certain of this. And he reveres paths, meaning the path we were on, the path we were set on in that moment deserved to see itself out. Every born inclination and emotion deserves a realization. That's something he would say. We were on the N2 and traffic was moving quickly. Part of me wanted to sit still and slow down, or crash to derail. We couldn't. The force surrounding us had become unbearable.

Langa is a township some miles from the city center of Cape Town. I had seen the townships coming and going from the airport, shantytowns where hundreds of thousands of the poorest of poor South Africans live. The houses are made of tin or wood, hacking into electricity poles that run sporadically across the expanse of it all. Everyone is fighting for survival. I didn't know exactly why so many people ended up there. I suppose it was cheap and I'm sure it had quite a bit to do with the apartheid but if I told you I gave a shit about their plight, that'd be dishonest and I don't believe in dishonesty. Mostly. What we were on our way to accomplish had little to do with them and everything to do with me.

We might as well have put lights and sirens on the top and sides of our car. The two of us were three-quarters white, and driving a white BMW M6 into the most dangerous section of Cape Town. We were also carrying something close to one million Rand – everything left from the Patricks' stash. It had been a while since we turned off the fringe and began to head for the center. Durban kept on repeating where he wanted to go, "The heart of this place, the heart, take us there." We were about to light a fire for the sake of lighting a fire. Both of us knew it.

When we got deep enough in, I told Burn to stop the car. Immediately, a group of children approached us, hands in front of their faces, holding air, moving their fingers up and down in rapid exaggerated motions. I asked Burn what they were doing and he said they were pretending to take pictures of us. I don't know how he knew, but that was exactly it. Cameras were their association to tourists in Langa. They came in their protected vans and took their pictures, collecting souvenirs and slum stories. Then they washed their hands and got the fuck out. I wanted to change that. When we stepped out of the car, they began reaching for our hands to shake, so untouched by the world surrounding them. It wasn't what I expected. Adults began gathering outside their homes, likely to talk over the two *idioots* who were going to get shot and made to disappear in their African hood. I knelt down and opened the briefcase, then handed 10,000 Rand to each of the six children. They looked at the money. When they looked back to me, I saw their eyes and felt like I'd robbed them of some form of ignorance or innocence before wondering if in every context, those words meant the same thing. The next moment, all six of them flew off to their guardians. Burn said something like we're fucked if we stay here. We moved.

I could hear a building commotion behind us. I could feel it. Something big was coming. We were moving fast but not fast enough, on foot down one of the narrow passageways. There were actual roads in the townships, at least on the outskirts, but everything leading in eventually narrowed and became all dirt and dust. I turned to Durban and told him I could feel my heart beating. He turned and nodded, sort of solemn because I could see there was definitely fear behind his mangled face. He smiled and mumbled. Maybe I should have been afraid too, or angry he had gotten us into what he did, or anything but what I was. I was just there.

Up ahead, there was an African man sitting outside one of the shacks. He was drinking out of an old paint can, smoking weed or a cigarette and once we got close, I saw he was wearing a Chicago Cubs hat. We came into view as he was taking a drink. The moment he saw us, he spat the swill in his mouth onto the dirt path. I asked if he spoke English. He nodded. I asked if we could come inside and pay to drink in his home. He was unsure, maybe because we were anything but cool and calm but probably because his eyes kept drifting to Durban and his Halloween mask of a face. He invited us inside. The man's name was Emmett. He had two children and they were huddled in a living space around a cracked television. Over my shoulder, through the window, I watched as our pursuing mob passed. There had to have been one hundred of them. Some were actually carrying pitchforks.

There was a large steel drum sitting in the corner of what I suppose could have been considered the living room. Emmett grabbed two paint cans that were hanging from the ceiling and handed one to Burn and the other to me. Then, he opened the steel drum and dunked our Langan chalices. I lifted the brew up to my nose. It smelled like turpentine at best. In contrast, if that moment had found us on the shores of Camps Bay eating caviar and drinking Cristal in the company of my recent and past, I would have already impaled myself. I raised the can to the ceiling with a toast before I took down the entire can, every drop. When I lowered the can and looked to Burn, I was and wasn't surprised to find him two sips behind. Burn and I shared a look of dismay, I think because we were both trying to cope with the chemical delirium flowing through our bodies when Emmett blew the tin roof off his shanty with this laugh I'll never forget, that bellowed from his guts and rushed through the holes of his rotted teeth. Once calm,

he shook his head and said, "Crazy men!" Then he followed suit and crushed his own pail. Then he dunked and filled all three. I didn't know how to tell him that one half gallon was plenty, or that the parasites in the drum and in my drink were already taking control of me, or that that day was going to be the first of the rest of his family's life. I just kept drinking.

It was either on the first round or second when Durban moved me. He raised his glass and said very casually, distantly, "May every day pain us, all the turns blind us, and never a moment escape." The day outside was dying and we were drunker than we should have been. We had met Emmett's two children. Thandiwe was a young boy, no older than 7. His father called him Tan. His eyes appeared with a strength and future I didn't see in his father. When I tried to shake his hand, he made me kneel. When I landed on the ground, he put his arms around me and gave me a hug. Tisha could have been no older than 4 and was so shy and beautiful. When Emmett tried to introduce her, she hid behind his legs, behind his shirt, anything that could playfully keep her from our sight. I became lost, put down my bucket of drink so that I could try and grasp exactly where I was, where I'd come from and what I'd done in the last 5 hours. When I found what I was grasping for, I leaned out and blinked it away, into the dirt and gone.

INSERT SKETCH: DURBAN HOLDING A PAINT CAN – SUN RAYS IN THE SHANTY – TAN LEANING AGAINST DURBAN'S LEG

Burn started playing this dancing game with the kids, I think because he was freaking the fuck out. Whatever it was, Tisha and Tan were into it, and began to mimic his flailing movement and wild sound. Soon, we were all yelling and dancing in circles, holding hands and laughing when Emmett's wife Malkia appeared in the doorway. Holy shit was our party over.

She silenced us all with her wide and ruby eyes, and explained that word had spread of two whites coming into Langa with a bag of stolen cash. She told us without remorse that we were going to get killed before, "Ignorant assholes! The world doesn't work the way you think it should…this is Africa…Langa!" She was in uniform with the name Nicholson on her lapel. It was one of the finest hotels in town. Clearly, she was put together. Absolutely, I was afraid of her. She walked to Emmett, changed language to Afrikaans and went fucking off, likely starting with his daytime drunk before moving into the impressions we'd leave on their impressionable children. I think we had broken every rule she had ever laid down for him. In that moment, a sobering feeling came over me. I began to think that maybe there was a possibility we were putting them in harm's way, that maybe she had every reason to be upset. That's when I cut in.

John moved to Emmett and Malkia and said, "It's true we came here to give out the money. There's close to one million Rand in this suitcase. I was going to spread it out but I don't want to do that anymore. I want to leave it all with you." There was a long beat, silence before Malkia wound up and slapped John across the face, and hard, creating an echo. Tisha began to cry and grabbed my hand. Malkia saw this. She stepped to the kitchen and grabbed a knife. I looked down to Tisha and told her everything was okay and that we were leaving. Then I looked to John, saw he wasn't finished. I can recall his words, word for word because everything he then said and did fully changed my perception of him. "I know you're proud…but you love your children…and love beats pride…I can see it I can feel it. You can take them away and you can have bright days or you can stay and have bright days but whatever choice you make you cannot in your right fucking mind deny me this." Then he told her with less eloquence that money is bullshit and we weren't leaving Langa with it. He said if they didn't take the money, we would walk the streets until someone found us, then, "If they kill us they kill us…me and Burn are dead soon anyway. At least this way, it'll be colorful, and today." His eyes stayed on Malkia, asking her if she would be ready for that, admitting then of a newfound love in his heart. He told her she would be responsible forever for extinguishing it. I think he was implying love for them. I think she understood. Malkia looked to Emmett and said something we didn't understand before he left the hut in a hurry and jogged away, down the path. She told us to sit, stabbed her knife into the wooden wall and asked if we were hungry. Durban actually said, "Whatchu got, mama?"

I sat gnawing on braai for some time. When I asked if it was dog, Malkia got angry, showed some humanity, and apologized to the family mongrel. There was so much edge in her. Even though we had settled down and become civil amongst one another, she was neither giving an inch nor taking any shit. At some point, I summoned the nerve to tell her she was my kind of girl. She shook her head, mildly incensed as I seemed to be concurrently gaining and losing ground with her. In those next 20 minutes, as we waited for Emmett, we didn't talk about the money at all. She asked about my face and I told her I'd gotten what I deserved and that people usually get what they deserve. The moment those words came out, I wished with all of my pathetic might that I could pull them back inside. It was too late.

Emmett finally came back and was stained with sweat under his neck and arms. Wherever he'd gone, he'd gone there running. He said, "The car stripped to bits. It is destined to Langa forever." Then he said his cousin would be there in moments, and that he had a car to take us back to Camps Bay. All we had to do was make it two hundred meters to the main road without being seen. I walked to

Malkia and stood in front of her. Then I told her I didn't believe in destiny or her God. She was a religious woman, apparent from the rosaries on her neck, on the necks of her children and hanging from the wall in her kitchen. I could feel her anger rising. Durban appeared certain she would keep the money. At that point, I wasn't sure. I felt the need to communicate something to everyone in that room, for us as much as them. I told Malkia however she chose to see us; there were infinite paths we could have found besides the one that brought us to her and her family. John had fallen for a girl whose husband smashed his face precisely enough to rock a form of guilt from his brain. One more hit and he would have been dead or in the hospital. One less and he'd have drunk or dropped until he blacked out on someone's street or beach or bathroom floor. Every day and moment and choice the two of us had covered and survived together had led us into the next. And all the beauty and shame we'd seen in the world that day and in our lives leading up to that day had delivered us. That's what I said, and that if we weren't the power she sought, the answer to all her prayers and her angels falling from the sky, then none of those things existed. After I finished, Durban leaned in and said something ridiculous and less subtle but I'm not going to repeat it.

We're on a mission from God. That's what I said. Ackroyd in Blues Brothers and I killed but the Africans didn't understand. Burn gave me this look because when he's heavy, I apparently can't be light. He was probably thinking of our getting torn to pieces by gunfire when we stepped out that door. Me...I was thinking high-speed getaway. A faint honk was coming from down the path, about two hundred meters away. Emmett said it was time to go. I moved in, said goodbye to Tisha and Tan and told them they were two of the more perfect things I'd ever seen. Burn did the same but in his own way. I shook Emmett's hand, took one last swig of the barreled booze, for luck, before I

took a running position by the door. Burn moved into Malkia and said something I couldn't hear. Her guard fell and she nodded. Then she unhooked the cross from around her neck and gave it to him. Burn moved to the door, turned to Tisha and Tan and asked them to count to three. Me and Burn traded smiles somewhere in the pause after two, with the bag remaining on the ground in the corner of the room.

I took my first step into the sunlight and everything went black. Then I was rolling in dirt, in pain. Blood was running down my face. There was a man standing over me with a gun pointed at Durban. He told Durban to get back inside and then dragged me in by a fistful of hair. In the corner of the room, Malkia had moved to stand in front of Tisha and Tan, to protect them. Emmett was talking with the man in Afrikaans, pleading with him. The man's eyes were bloodshot and his arms were shaking, not from fear, but from something far less predictable. When Emmett said something the man didn't like, he pointed the gun at the children. Malkia screamed and started to cry.

Burn stood with blood falling in tributaries from a hole in his forehead. He appeared a demon. The man quickly pointed the gun at Burn and told him not to move. Still, Burn edged closer. The man raised the gun to Burn's head and Malkia turned away to shield the children, so they wouldn't see him die. I screamed but it was too late. The trigger had been pulled, but the bullet didn't fire. Burn got control and became insane, pinning the man against the floor. The gun was in Burn's hand, and his blood was dripping onto the man's snarling face, into his mouth as he looked up. Through Emmett's translation, the man said, "Go. Leave where you don't belong. When you look back, the children's throats will be cut first. I will take everything." There was another honk coming from down the road when Burn looked up to me and said, "Go Durban." I hesitated and he screamed it. As I jogged out the door and looked over my shoulder, Burn was dragging the man between rows of shanties, until they were out of sight. No one was outside, so I kept running, towards the waiting car. It was quiet, save my footsteps, until I heard two pops behind me. I saw our car ahead and dove into the back seat as a new stranger covered me with a blanket and told me to stay down. He started to drive away. I told him he had to wait. He was afraid. I put my hand on his arm and gripped it. I told him my friend was still outside, and that he was coming, and that I could not leave without him. Another minute passed before Burn dove in and we finally pulled away. Longest minute of my life.

We got to a house away from the Patricks and the air was cold. It was quiet in the hills above the city and I was out back watching the sky. Burn appeared. He wouldn't sit. He just stood there looking out at the moon on the ocean. I asked if he was okay and he didn't speak. I told him there were no mistakes anymore. His gaze fell and he nodded. Then he said, "Yeah." His voice broke but there were no tears. Somewhere inside, he must have been in a great deal of pain. I wanted to feel it. Maybe that's why I didn't move, and remained by his side until the sun came up, long after he had given up trying to gain a composure we both knew would never return.

Part Two

LOS ANGELES
October 22, 2007

After Cape Town, I came home to Los Angeles. I moved into an old friend's empty apartment just north of Sunset in West Hollywood. I brought my things inside, all of it in two hands, and almost immediately wanted to abandon again. I told myself to slow down, to be done using, to stop needing to be anywhere else, everywhere but where I was, all the time. It had been months since John and I last spoke to or saw each other. Maybe it was better that way. Still, I was afraid of what I would become without Durban. Parts of me were in trouble. And things were getting worse.

I met someone Durban knew named Benny for lunch at Chateau Marmot. It was one in the afternoon and I spotted him right away. He was a round, mentioned Brit, and appeared a bespoke suited slob. The waiter was dropping a second martini at his table when he looked up and figured me too, flipping his hand to invite me over. He looked bothered to be there, or bothered I wasn't someone more. When I sat down he shook my hand and said, "John sent me some of your work, some travel rag garbage and said I had to meet you. He's going to be worth a billion dollars someday, so here I am." Then, "You're lucky I'm indebted to him else I would have been gone. You're twenty late, derelict junkie." He seemed committed to a rant about my wasting his time when I cut him off sharply. Benny said, "Alright alright, nobody likes a touchy prick." Then he sighed and asked if I had something for him. I had written about the time Durban and I spent in Berlin and Cape Town, mostly to process. Then I showed the pages to Durban. I thought maybe Durban needed to process himself. Durban told me to bring the pages to Benny. Reluctant, I pulled the pages out of my pocket and passed them across the table. Benny put his glasses on and started reading. At times over the course of those fifteen or twenty minutes, he would get through reading something and look up to judge me before his eyes returned to the pages. Then he got to the end and flipped them onto the table. And he just sat there. Then he said, "You can write a bit. Not much, but enough." He took a long drink of water before starting again, "You're aware this is perhaps the most trite subject matter in the history of life, or literature. Coined by assholes and desperates since the beginning of time?" Then mockingly, "Rule today as if it's your last, as if dying tomorrow would be alright because you lived it, man. You lived it!" He sat back and laughed, calculating. Then, "Do you know why John came to me? If he wanted you published to be published, he could write me a check. The world hasn't changed so much. Money still buys everything. But he knows I will not take his money. And I will not put something into the world that I feel does not belong. Do you understand?" I nodded, catching up with Durban's plans as Benny spoke them aloud. Benny continued, "This thing you're doing here, it's a noble effort. Unfortunately, if I made time for every noble effort in my life I wouldn't be much the man. Good day Mr. Winburn." He threw a fifty, stood, and was halfway to the lobby door when he slowed to a stop. Then he just stood there. He turned around and walked back to the table. At some point during his exit, he must have realized. He said, "John Durban is one fucked bloke. I only say that because…this is real, isn't it?" I didn't say anything. To be honest, I didn't know for sure. He quickly rifled through the pages again, "This is real. There are other things. Cape Town. You're a bloody killer…" I put my hand up to stop the word, but it was too late. He put the pages down and left, but not before, "We'll be in touch, Mr. Winburn. Try and clean yourself up a bit."

…

Though she was the last thing I should have wanted, I thought about Michelle every day since the two of us left each other. I was better because of her, formed, for the short time we spent together. She was my hand in the dark. When I found myself on the brink of doing something I might regret, I'd sit down and write to her for hours without intention of ever delivering a word, pages upon pages until something inside of me tamed, and I could move on properly with my life. Pure madness. My whole body ached for her. When I couldn't look at the notebooks any longer, I brought them to the roof and set them on fire. Then I watched them burn. When the fire had died out and all that remained was a crude ash, I walked back to the apartment and slept like I used to, before I was ever disturbed by sickness, or death, or Durban.

One morning, I woke to a doorbell and found Michelle standing on my front step. She took a breath, as if to prep and summon courage before she said, "There's only one rule. We say everything." I wanted to touch her, but she would not yet allow it. I wanted to fall into her, but the space between us was too thick. So I just began talking, saying everything. I told her about growing up with my brother in the suburbs of Chicago. I had a path I could follow. My parents both worked jobs and raised us with love across the years, through schools and seasons. Every once in a while, someone close to us would die – an uncle from leukemia, a grandparent from cirrhosis. There would be a funeral, and remembrances, and from a young age, I felt I had a handle on death. Then a shift began. In seventh grade, two girls I knew were killed in a hit and run. One of them was my first crush. Sophomore year, a friend of mine hung himself. He was the happiest guy I knew. Some years later, I lost my brother. My parents lost hope. Paths dissolved. I left Chicago and moved to Los Angeles because it felt like an escape. But it wasn't. So I ran to Europe and met Durban. I told her things had gotten out of control. I told her I killed a man. She stood there. I told her I put a gun to the bottom of his head and pulled the trigger. I told her I could still feel his blood on me, and that I felt ruined. I cried. I looked down at my hands. They were shaking. There was a voice inside that begged me to send her off, to make her go. It said, "Tell her about Berlin. That'll do it." But I couldn't. I wasn't strong enough. I asked about her fiancé and she said, "It's over. You never kissed me." I reached out to take her hand. She let me, and took mine. She smiled, easy as always. Then I kissed her, sat and listened as she spent the next two hours saying everything.

The first week was hard, but she never left my side. I told her about Durban and learned about her life abroad. She had been living with her father in Sydney from the age of seven into her early teens. When he got too busy with work and travel and she began to feel alone in a faraway country, she said goodbye and moved home to live with her mother and stepfather in San Diego. There, she fell in love with the ocean and a boy who would ultimately propose. And she fell in love with art. One morning when I was sick, she asked if she could draw a portrait of me on the bed. I agreed. It was one of the most honest things I had ever seen. Right now in the living room, there are two more. One is a cityscape of Hollywood looking down from the top of Yamashiro during a hazy sunset. The other is of a mother and child standing alone in the middle of a weekend crowd on the Venice boardwalk, holding balloons and laughing. When she's done with a piece, she often puts it out on the street, leaning it against a random stop sign or building. Last week, I saw a painting of hers hanging in a Silver Lake gallery and sold for eight thousand dollars.

Two months after I was clean, we went out to eat on 3rd street to celebrate her first officially booked job as an illustrator. She was hired for nineteen drawings that would compliment the book of a famous British children's author. We were almost finished with dinner when some girl came out of the darkness to lean over the sidewalk railing and to put her face on my cheek. She stood back and smiled, awaiting a great reception. I was certain I knew her but couldn't place who she was. Her gaze grew toxic when she had to remind me. It was Naomi, the girl I left when I first left Los Angeles – the girl who followed me by Durban's phone calls to Paris. I never thought of myself as someone so forgetful. I had never been before and quickly wondered what that revealed. It was like my mind or heart had cleaned me out and decided to only allow my attention to be drawn to dire and necessary things for the remainder of my stay. She was neither.

I was watching Michelle talk to Naomi and I didn't like it. Or what's better, I didn't know how to handle seeing both of them occupy the same space. Naomi was so rigid. All I could think of was how a girl, or anything so impactful could become so disposable. It should have been tragic, but wasn't. When I came out of thought, Michelle was talking about her decision to leave school to focus on, "Other things." Naomi was taking her in, wondering I think, how serious the two of us were. When Naomi arrived at an understanding she didn't like, her emotions spun, cutting Michelle off abruptly, purposefully. She mentioned she'd been following my writing in magazines and online. Naomi then gave what seemed to be a false commendation for my finally doing something real, as if she were an authority, and said we should catch up over a drink sometime. I nodded, maybe more indifferently than was intended, causing her to storm off with two guys she had introduced and were standing there, oddly, for the couple minutes it took for all of this to play out. When she was gone, Michelle leaned across the table, took my hand and kissed me. I remember feeling so content in the moment, so comfortable. But it was more than that. When we went home that night, I was twenty-six and realized I'd never truly been able to understand the word love until Michelle came to face me. I no longer had any use for the word. People in town who had no reason to know my work seemed to know it in the coming weeks, when a story I wrote, "Love is Dead," was published in a popular online magazine, inspired by events occurring that night. The piece was optioned and fast-tracked as a romantic comedy at one of the major studios. Someone accomplished was hired to write the screenplay. Things were happening.

Attempts at contact with Durban were made when I was on his side of the world. As Michelle and I made trips to the Mediterranean and Tuscany, he and I were in constant but impersonal contact through texts and e-mails. I told him where we were going to be and he'd respond late. Or he'd be enthusiastically vague. By the time he would make a claim to come around, we'd be long gone. At some point I made clear that I would have no problem walking out on my own, the thing hanging over us. Whatever it turned out to be. I wasn't going to will John Durban back into existence or steady him to remain by my side. With Michelle, I had everything I needed.

...

My dear Los Angeles. Don't get me wrong. I've grown comfortable here and this is my home. Truth, I'll never be able to live in another city in the states. This town grows and wraps itself around you. Its roots plunge. People come here to live forever, to chase immortality in the form of art or entertainment. They're wide-eyed and glowing and hopeful and I like to think of it like this – once a year in Los Angeles, the rain comes relentless for a week. The hills mudslide. Dirty streets become slick and if you're here to witness it, the entire production comes off as nothing short of the end of the world. Every year at the time of the floods, there's mass exodus. I think of flooding waters as the dreams of thousands rushing down the streets, shooting off and disappearing into the gutters, becoming chemical runoff on the way to the ocean. Immortality isn't for the faint of heart. Those that leave here leave empty, and those that remain likely and slowly become forgotten, their dreams forgotten, and the more they realize it, the deeper they fall, sinking this city like a plague, pulling against the buoyant few. I've struggled and now I'm not. I've been broken and now I'm not. I've found my path again. Depending on the hour, I either see myself as the problem, or a solution.

AMALFI
January 25, 2008

I've been not attentive. Time just goes. I remember South Africa like it was yesterday, living with Burn and feeling clear, clearer than I had been in a very long time. Possibly ever. Sure, we had some alarming adventures, but the majority of the time we spent together in that golden city was fucking solid. And I felt like I was just beginning to understand the meaning of things before he left. From Cape Town, I fell into old habits, spending my months in Monaco, New York, Vienna, Hong Kong. Every city became a new disappearing act, avoidance of a lurking shadow. Then out of nowhere, something happened.

I met her in transit, in Frankfurt when we were both on layover. This Jenny. I don't remember what we started talking about, or where or why…all I remember was the feeling of her beside me, and that every word out of her mouth was so scorching, I ignored my flight and paid strict attention to the only feeling that had mattered in months – wherever I was going wouldn't suffice without her. That's what I said before we bought new tickets and then flew to St. Tropez for twelve days.

Imagine a girl standing in the middle of a crowded street in the South of France, French cars and drivers stacked for blocks and miles, the sun against her skin, hands running through her hair, white dress floating against the sea breeze and silence, not a soul asking her to move for fear of something they could not define. Imagine her being yours, instantly, deserved or not, for reasons that could never be explained. Imagine taking her, holding her, looking into her, expecting light and seeing something the opposite, void, like a mirror, and falling into it. Imagine her not speaking of it, ever. Imagine time disappearing. Becoming lost. Imagine her as an addiction, saying, "You think you have control. That's the difference between us. I am going to take everything from you. This isn't just going to end. It's going to end badly." Imagine a boy believing her every word. Rooting for her, begging her to try, to take him apart, to unmake him. She had a shadow too. Imagine that.

We were staying at a house in St. Tropez. A friend of mine owned it. He was a high-end, high-volume art dealer and seemed to be incarcerated somewhere. When I wrote him from the airport in Frankfurt, his assistant told me the door was open and the house would be empty for a long time. I couldn't recall what had made this friend into a friend I could go to if I ever needed what I needed, a place where I could set up shop and devour a single living being for an extended period of time. All I had to go on was the note attached to his name in my phone, "Paranoid, not fun or cool lunatic – owes big – palace in St. Tropez – be sure he's not there." That's how me and Jenny ended up in his house for as long as we did. The days and mornings and nights bled into one slow moving mass, highlighted by crisis as frequent as the tide rolling in, rolling out. My memory of it is so vivid...

The night she first revealed herself, she wanted Italian, light Italian with a bottle of Rose. Something we could have against the setting sun. She was like that, always looking for moments or things in the natural world that she described as, "Keeping the world from falling." Then she said, "Like you," and a fucking shockwave blew through my body. She reached across the table and took my hand, with actual lightning in her hand. There was fire burning inside of her eyes. I could feel myself going mad, holding her hand, always afraid of the next moment and of how she might use it to slip away. I remember my fear for what was inevitably coming. That was Jenny. My need was to protect us.

She was mine because from the moment we met, I had no choice. She said I'm yours.

We were walking home on opposite sides of the street after she had kissed me once, twice, before a distance grew inside of her and then between us. I could see it happening. Her mind was under attack. There were kids in the road playing and lovers wandering. I could see the moment she passed them or anything living, this transference of darkness that made her so beautiful to me, but would violate joy and comfort from the world around her, from the kids, from the lovers. The scene appeared magnificent and a nightmare at once.

We got home that night and she threw her things onto the counter. I hovered over her, watching her and saying nothing. I asked if she was okay and she looked over at me and said yes. The way she said it was all hers – both incredulous that I would think to ask, and a lie. She came into me then, hard and panting. Then she was on top of the counter, a large wooden island in the middle of the kitchen and I was there too, inside of her, pants trapping my ankles because anything else wouldn't have been soon enough. She was ready so fast, whispering in my ear, "With me, with me." I don't know what was keeping me back, instinct for what would eventually become of us, fascination, fear for her, fear of her, fear that I was maybe making this force or vendetta between her and the world much worse. When she began her tilt, I followed. I pressed into her as we came, as she held the back of my head with just her nails and breathed fire. There was a quiet moment, but only one before she pushed me off then moved away, out of the kitchen without a word.

There were noises coming from down the hall, doors and drawers and closets opening and closing, objects falling to the floor. I sat there and listened. She was looking for something. Thinking back on the night, I should have leapt in and cut her off. Because I knew the look in her eye when she walked out of the room. Very suddenly, the noises stopped. I stood to follow her path down the hallway. There was another distinct noise, one I immediately feared to be the twirling cylinder of a gun. Of course when it came to Jenny, I always feared the worst, and didn't actually think she was going to be holding a revolver until I turned the corner to find her holding a revolver. Five bullets fell to the ground and scattered. She was looking at the barrel before the cylinder spun again, before a tight whip of her hand threw it back in. She looked to me then. I knew what came next.

I reached to take the gun and she said, "Spin if you want to," light and easy like she was talking about the weather. Adrenaline flooded my body and my sight narrowed. I thought I was about to go blind from panic, maybe because my body was also trying to disassociate or remove me from the events that were about to follow. I was about to have a one in six chance of blowing a hole in my head. I didn't care about that as much as I cared about what my own survival might do to the probability of hers. I thought of the bullet doing its job, taking her life and leaving me there alone, having survived, looking at her dead body. Of course I thought of taking the gun and running away with it, of removing it and saving us. Of course I did. But I knew if that happened, she would be gone, probably in the middle of the night, and that I would never see her again. I put the barrel to my head. Her face was calm. I pulled the hammer into a hollow snap as a flash of white and its echoes surged my senses. Empty chamber. I was still alive, still living. That moment, I saw Jenny in a new light, believed that I understood her more than anyone ever could, and that I could save her. Every day we spent together, her ill desire only grew. I thought if only I could explain myself, if only I could convey everything properly, all of her pain might go away. I lowered the gun, so I could say everything she needed to hear. But then I couldn't say anything. Words would not arrive, so I gave her the gun.

She wouldn't look at me, only down, aroused before, "Spin, or as is?" I said nothing. I couldn't feel my pulse. I couldn't breathe. She put the gun to her head and looked at me. I remember being so certain she was about to die. Instead, there were two clicks. I was biting down so hard on my front tooth that it snapped as a click inside of my head. She pulled the trigger, click two the hammer through an empty barrel. I could feel blood collecting in my mouth, pooling as I watched her convulse, scream, raise the gun, and fire against two empty chambers before the third chamber's bullet exploded into the ceiling. The gun fell from her hand and onto the floor. I spit a mouthful of blood across the room and away from her as she moved into me, my pain already numb, my tongue revealing razor ivory and hanging nerve. I wondered how long I had before we faced it all again, and if I would ever have the words to stop her.

We spent the night there on the floor. She asked me to hold her tight, then tighter, always tighter, never tight enough. Looking down the hall, I could see the light of the moon. It was so close. I wanted to pull us into it, beneath it, to be encompassed by it, thinking it could somehow protect us, shield us from my fear of everything unknown and approaching. We were too fragile to move.

...

One morning, we were waiting to be picked up from the harbor in Sorrento. I asked Jenny if she had any friends in Italy and she brushed me off, small talk, something I could give a fuck about before the conversation became something else entirely, because of the way she handled me, because there was a pattern of response she gave after any potentially meaningful question I asked, like the girl was so beyond everything, or had so fucking much to hide. That's why I pushed. She said, "Fine, if that's what you want John, we'll meet my friends." Very flat. Her phone rang as a white boat with high arching sails glided in. We walked to meet it. There was a young man at the helm about my age, who was straddling the dock and boat as we approached, holding them together so we could jump on. Once aboard, I watched the two of them embrace, good and long before he pulled back, looked at her and said, "Love you baby, I've missed you." He turned to me then, shook my hand quickly, "Romero." We were guided to the front of the boat before Romero jumped to the back, kicked us from the dock and shouted, "To Capri!"

Romero was southern Italian, born and raised. I gathered quickly he went back far with Jenny, probably as far as anyone. But even he hadn't seen her in a long time. Right away, I understood he was going to be important. He was yelling things from behind the wheel, mostly English and some Italian that would make Jenny laugh, then turn to me and say, "Don't worry. It's not about you, John Durban." She was considerate and hateful. I wanted to burn them to the ground, everything that could separate the two of them from me. Once the boat cleared the harbor, Romero brought out an open bottle of Champagne. He poured a glass for the two of us and one for himself. We drank to something but I don't remember what it was, because I was watching Jenny, listening to the way she spoke to him. I was searching for something, an anchor, something that could hold her against the world and in my mind. Because up until that point, we were only ever barely hanging on. That's why I was pushing us into the things we were about to do – sit down like pretend civilized people, with actual other people, in an actual civilized setting Romero called, "The famed Caprisian villa." That way, maybe I could at least catch a glimpse. Maybe I could understand a sliver of what had made her.

We were approaching the marina on Capri when Jenny's tone and shape shifted. She was cowering. She looked right at me while motioning out to sea and said, "Keep going. Anywhere but here." Romero laughed. I knew she wasn't joking. He admitted the boat was a borrowed prop to impress her, and that it had to be returned. Jenny sat back. The only thing left was for me to find the most secluded and empty spot on the island and take her there, make it ours and apologize for ever considering anything else. Those words were honestly on the tip of my lips. As I moved in to tell her, close enough to feel her breathing, she looked through me and said, "I know what you think you're doing. I promise. You will lose. We are not the same." With that, my sympathy left. I called her darling and told her she didn't know a fucking thing about me.

Romero's car was parked in the marina lot. We drove the slants and cliffs to a villa on the southeastern coast overlooking the Faraglioni. There was a gate with armed guards. Romero revealed it to be the home of his lover. When Jenny asked the name, Romero replied, "Luciano." I remember liking Romero a great deal more after hearing he had likely not fucked her. We entered the grounds and Luciano approached. He embraced Romero with a kiss before introducing himself, before taking us to a table in the back yard, where eight people were already sitting, drinking in their ridiculous huge floral hats and dressed to mime a campaign they had probably seen in summer Vogue. They were laughing, cackling, drunken. The scene was gross. Jenny stopped and took my hand, turned me to face her, making me believe for moments of a coming peace or reconciliation before, "Was I not enough?" Something in me wilted before we separated and she introduced herself to the entire table, a stranger to all but Romero. He was all she had. I knew then I had fucked up, and that I would pay for it. We were seated in the middle of the table and on opposite sides, divided by harsh marble and my poor miscalculation. Once everyone was settled, Luciano raised a glass and began toasting the day. The whole time, Jenny was so cool, such a liar. Luciano was still speaking when I stood, became silent when I walked around the table to stand over Jenny and ask very audibly if we could get the fuck out of there. I was stern and panicked enough that no one thought it was a joke. She said, "Sit down."

There was a staff of people serving us. They were circling always, always pouring drinks, removing and replacing plates and glasses and bottles. They were manic. I couldn't eat. I wasn't hungry and felt sick. It was the tone of their voices. It was their collective and detached banter. It was the shame I felt. No, it was the way her eyes had been looking at me all afternoon, unforgiving. The light outside was bright and blinding, the world overexposed. There were fucking assholes everywhere but especially by my sides, two Englishmen who claimed to have known me from somewhere. They wanted to talk about my father and his prospects that would soon become mine, about some financial windfall happening back in London that I should have been in on. I told them several times, exactly, I do not fucking care what you are talking about and we are not engaged in a conversation. My eyes were on Jenny. She was effortless across the table, speaking in Italian to three women huddled around her. They were all laughing and enchanted. On the surface, she made it all look so simple, knowing I was watching, knowing I was thinking how much less capable I was than her. She wanted me to see something, that I had no control, especially over her, and never would. Great fear swept over me. The English were still spitting as they spoke, too beside themselves to understand my imaginings of hacking their scalps off one at a time, with dull rocks in my bare hands. I stared at Jenny with a desperation until she excused herself with a glance, and was gone. When I stood to follow, Romero cut me off, grabbed hold of my arm and said, "Okay, okay. Time we know more of each other."

We stood on a cliff over the Tyrrhenian. He said, "I knew today wasn't real. But I was watching. Because I care about her more than you could know. Tell me, what ever lead you to believe you could take her on like this?" I didn't answer. Romero was living in Cetara when they first met, in a small house his parents had left for him. He said he was nineteen, driving back from Naples when he saw a girl hitching on the side of the road. There was a power in her, something undeniable that pulled him over. She stayed with him for a year. He said, "Of course there was a story. But I didn't force her to tell it." He took this deep breath like he was about to say something very important before it seemed he gave up on the thought altogether. He patted my shoulder and said, "If I didn't like you, I wouldn't be saying anything. But she is better. I can see that." When he began to repeat himself, I knew he was stalling. When I ran off he yelled, "Let her go!"

I stormed into the house after her, looking everywhere. I approached the staff, demanding. No one knew anything. I ran to the front gate. The guard told me she left with a driver, asked to be taken back to the marina. There were no other cars so I stole one, a Bentley with keys in the ignition. When I got to the marina, I searched and couldn't find her. A very real paranoia began to escalate inside of me. If she beat me back to the car in Sorrento, I would never see her again.

I would never be able to say what I needed to say, that I fucked up, and that I was sorry. There was a cigarette boat in the harbor that I also tried to steal before the owner stopped me and threatened to call the police before accepting a huge cash bribe to literally fly me across the water, back to the marina in Sorrento. All told, I was standing next to the car within 30 minutes. Thirty minutes later and from a hundred meters away, I could see her approaching against the dark. When she was close enough to flip me the keys, she did, brushing past before lifting her legs over the door and lowering into the passenger seat. I got in and said nothing, not a word, thinking of silence as peace. It wouldn't last.

We were winding the coast of Amalfi in her old Alfa Romeo, topless, trying to hit the equivalent of a hundred miles an hour between the nagging turns, the high and jagged cliffs. Her mouth was pressing my ear, screaming about inevitability and of all things expiring, every word out of her poetic and redundant, insane because the ride, like everything when it came to Jenny, could have been anything but what it was. Instead of just hearing her and listening to everything I deserved and provoked that day, I instead fell into it, her trap, and began screaming back, possessed by obsession. We were a great contradiction – meant to be, meant to destroy. I wanted to jerk the wheel, to please her, to miss a turn, to plow through the guardrails so we could attempt flight and fail. Anything together. I could feel adrenaline like mercury rising into my teeth, readying me over and again before a guiding voice would silence me, his hand steadying. It was Burn. I could hear his reasoning, that it couldn't end like that. Driving off a cliff by my own hand wasn't the path. It wouldn't be acceptable, and I wouldn't be forgiven for it. Not ever. Between her screams, between her pleading, there would be moments when I could see something in her eyes I knew only existed within a handful of people in the entire world – she was truth, authentic to the bone. She wanted me to do it, to take us both. And I wanted so badly to show her how capable I was, to prove myself, to have that control, to feel the touch of her hand to mine as we fell and shared the last fear. But I couldn't. So instead I pulled the wheel right, settled on compromise and drove our dysfunction straight into an Amalfi rock wall.

INSERT SKETCH: DURBAN AND JENNY CRASHED – CAR SMOKING – THE MOON

It was quiet and the car was fucked. The road was silent and still. I didn't know how long we had been sitting there, unconscious or collecting, but when I came back, Jenny was slumped against the dashboard. I remember that sight of her being the most frightening of my life. Then, like a miracle, she resurrected, sat up and turned to me with a new lightness. There was blood running through her hairline, polluting her dark strands. She laid her hand across my face and told me she loved me – the first and only time I had ever wanted to hear it from anyone like her. It started to rain as we fucked on the back hood of that dead car. Every moment, every movement served to stab me through. Screams of internal injury. As the rain soaked her hair, and softened all wounds, I could see diluted streams of blood rolling down her precious face. Her eyes became so clear. The trouble had left. We hitched a ride to Positano, got a room with a view and stayed in bed for three days, hands and limbs twisting as more rains fell and our bodies tried to heal. I believed, actually believed I'd found the end of what I was and the beginning of something new.

I woke the fourth day to a blinking light on the phone, orange or yellow, alone. On the message she said, "Good morning John." There was a terribly long pause, so long I worried she had given up or that the machine dropped her call. I remember falling to my knees before she continued, "I don't want you to think I didn't stop at the door to weigh you, and us, because I know you think about things like that. I did stop. And I meant what I said, everything I ever said. You told me you understood me and that whatever I had to give was what you would take. But that's not good enough. Not for you. Not for me. We don't belong together. Or to each other. Or to anything." Her voice cracked. She apologized for her dark tones, her always dark tones before, "I'm gone to save you John Durban. I beg you stay away."

LONDON HEATHROW
August 29, 2008

It was the day of my twenty-seventh. I was in town for a story Benny had set up for me. I'd also been trying to get a hold of John for three days, to put to rest what could only be described as fear of facing one another. He wasn't returning my calls, or e-mails, or texts – not one. I gave up, told him when I was flying out and even the flight number as a last ditch so he knew exactly when I would be leaving my hotel. Still, I didn't hear a word. I let him and everything go, decided the two of us weren't meant for anything any longer, and that I was going on alone. That's when I heard the idiot rumblings of a voice behind me, in song. I didn't even turn to look. Didn't have to. It grew and was growing, echoing through the terminal. Durban was carrying a Cinnabon in his hand, and it was on fire because he'd taken the cardboard from a roll of paper towels and fashioned it into a torch that was turning wild. The flames must have burnt his hand because he shouted and dropped the entire presentation onto the floor. Then he shuffled away like it wasn't his. Empty handed, he sang louder. Then, he commanded the entire immediate terminal to join. For him, they always obliged.

It had been two years since I met Burn in Paris, two fucking years. Before I left for Heathrow, I actually debated whether or not I was going to go, because in our case I knew it would be easier to barely miss each other for the rest of our lives. I thought about sitting at home and falling asleep, letting his time in London pass and the excuses I would conjure to cover my cowardice, excuses he would certainly see through. He was on the edge of dismissing me I could feel it. I think that's what ultimately delivered me to him, a certain fear of abandonment. I was so glad to walk up to his sweet face and into his accepting arms. After all, it was his birthday. He looked like a different man. We had much to discuss.

I'm not sure what I was readying for exactly when I saw him coming. He had that look of when we first met, like he was rabid and about to kiss my cheek and claw off my face. It was so initially stunning to me, both in that moment and two years before, that I found myself caught in a realization that I'd been underestimating him. As far as I'd felt I'd come in my own right, and as far as I could feel he'd come in two years, one thing had remained that was as true then as in the moment I first met him – Durban is like no body or thing. He is a walking storm; the kind that comes late at night and comfortably rattles the world. He was talking a thousand miles an hour, protocol for John in rare, uncomfortable situations. He does this to remove what he calls composed thought but in my case it was being done to remove the possibility of confronting him on where he had been all the times I came calling. I cared but couldn't. At the point we had reached, it didn't matter anymore. And anyway, we had better things to talk about, like what was keeping John Durban clear-headed near midnight on a Friday in London. He looked younger, vibrant, like he'd peeled away five years of hard living. If he was still on the corrupting shit he'd been on in the past, he was dialing it back. He looked good. The sight of him gave me hope, primer for what I was about to do.

We walked to the end of the terminal, found two seats at the last open bar in Heathrow. It was clear the bartender was closing and ready to go home for the night. She got upset when we walked up, not about to let her go. John said it best, we had much to discuss. He looked at her like he does them all. From across the bar he said, "Come here please." She did. They always did. Then, "I can see you're upset, but you need to stop that and be supportive. This is Burn, my dearest friend in the world. All I need is for you to treat us with great care. I promise I will make it worth your while." Hearing the words dearest friend in the world made me uncomfortable. He told her it was my birthday, dropped one thousand pounds on the bar, then another, then ten more. She closed the doors and turned off the lights, made three drinks then another three, let Durban connect my iPod to the stereo dock and that's how the night began.

I brought up Michelle. Burn had been living with her and writing about her for some time. Hearing him speak of their greatness made me feel like I'd missed out, or that I was a bad person for not recognizing and paying more attention. They were very serious, be-all end-all serious, and she sounded good for him. I knew about the paths Burn had been cutting for Benny in Los Angeles and in parts of the world. I'd been keeping up, reading everything that was going out with his name on it. And I was impressed. The seed had sprouted. He was evolving into something good, a genuine article. Most of the pieces he wrote centered on a figure he'd call Girl, a mentioned tribute to me. I thought for a while that she was some fictitious thing, a central figure to fill a need in his mind because he's like that. At some point, he tried to change the subject from Michelle to the full confession I'd recently written him about Jenny and Amalfi. But I resisted. I needed us to be bigger than two guys falling into similar patterns, talking about shit like pain, maybe because I already knew so much about the two of them from his writing and vice-versa, but also because I didn't want to talk about my abandoning bitch and all the trouble she'd been causing me.

There was something disturbing in John that needed prying. As good as he thinks he is at keeping what he calls his shit from me, the effort is always obvious. For obvious reasons, I can guarantee that unless they're being paid by the hour, John has no one to pry for him. He had recently written me about this girl he met and remained with for a stretch of time around Europe – Jenny from Amalfi. Whatever was happening between them was setting a precedent for John. She was all I wanted to talk about. We were sitting at the bar and he was being evasive, knowing I had read everything he sent, and that I knew how harmed he was by her, especially still. The biggest problem I had with Durban was that he wouldn't own anything. He wouldn't talk about why he had been avoiding me and wouldn't acknowledge the damage she had done. At that point in our relationship, these actions were unforgivable.

The day she left, I tried to brush it off, tried to move around and pretend everything was working. Fucking liar. I found her father and tried to pretend what he told me, to lock her away and honor her and forget her, was working. Fucking liar. I tried to tag us as a casual and glancing encounter, like the dozens I'd recently had, like the low thousands I'd likely had in my life. Fucking liar. I couldn't fool myself. The first week, she pulled at me, hard and constantly. After that, her pulls turned ripping, destroying, possessing. She's living inside of me. That's what I said to Burn. All I wanted was to leave Heathrow, to find my flat and stay inside of it until I or the poison inside of me expired. I told Burn I hadn't seen or heard from her since she left and how everything just went quiet. I told him how badly I wanted to see her alive, her eyes, her existence, anything that was concrete and not like some disappearing fucking mist, anything real to substitute everything that's been created and is being created inside of my mind. He just looked at me, nodding, ordering drinks as I told the story in person, the behind the scenes that made up those weeks of my life she fucking hijacked. I admitted disbelief, that me and Jenny could have had what we had and it not be real or something worth fighting for. My vehicle had been built strong, ironclad, and since the morning I woke up without her and every morning after, the thought of her penetrates, all the way through. I've a talent I'm no longer proud of, ability to look another human in the eyes, and help them believe anything I want them to believe. To bend and mold them into whatever shape I

choose, for however long I choose. It's why I could have anyone, why I could disclose a resume of the women I've been with and inspire global disbelief. So when this situation with Jenny makes me wonder whether she was simply turning the trick back on me, which is the only explanation I can come up with to make the two of us make sense in my mind, I'm flooded with hatred then admiration, then a desperate fucking obsession to sit down and study the subject with a new and careful brand of respect. The things I'd do to see her one more time.

Durban was not well. I kept feeding him drinks to soften him up, to get him going, then to keep him going. Nothing made sense in his mind, but especially the possibility that someone could do to him what he'd all along been doing to the world. I didn't think he could ever become affected by someone the way he was. I wished I could have met her. He was describing her and every word was so eloquent and dismantling, circling my mind, forming this image of living, walking fire. He was doing this overprotective thing, speaking fast and staggered to shield himself from the full-blown admission that a living thing had gotten the best of him. At a point, we were above that. The shape she left him in was a contradiction. This was a man who, for the first twenty-seven years of his life, had been in total control of a carefully assembled emotionless state. No more.

I don't remember what I was talking about, just that I was talking about something awful, just to hear myself speak when Burn cut me off and was very stern about it. He looked at me with threatening eyes and said, "Let her go. There's something about this one. As your friend, I'm telling you."

I told him he was John Durban, and I don't know if it was the way I said it that set him over the edge, but he stood, slapped his heart hard and fast – appearing moved. He came into me and took me into his arms with this great and voluminous hug, like I had given him exactly what he needed in that moment. I caught our bartender looking on with a smile, who Durban named Angie Live after the song he kept playing. I smiled back until John pulled away. It was four in the morning and we had to finally go. As a parting gift, Angie Live gave us a bottle and kicked us out. She asked who we were. John told her, "Durban and Burn." As if she should have known all along.

We were walking down the empty terminal with a bottle of Jack, an iPod dock and speaker we had stolen with permission from the bar, and Burn's suitcase. I was carrying Burn's suitcase, like a gentleman. We were light and free and easy before all of that ended and I felt something coming. When it came to having someone I wanted beside me, my instincts of them leaving had evolved into a razor sharpness.

Durban was three steps behind when the words sort of dribbled out, "You're about to leave me. I mean, really leave me." I turned, thinking he was trying to be funny before I remembered he was exactly right, that what I had set out to do in London was sever the association between the two of us so that I could go on alone. I was about to say goodbye to John Durban forever.

He started coming up with this rationale...things about my fear and my instability, not being able to rely on me like he needed to. He said he loved me like a brother...that he loved me like a fucking brother, then, "My shit is mine and I'm sorry I pulled you in. I'm sorry I couldn't control myself that night. You have this over you now and I'm so sorry. But the rest of the way I have to go alone." I struggled for words. He told me he had no choice. I asked what he expected me to do. I started pleading, confessions of movement towards something important I couldn't define. I said cutting me off would kill that. I could hear the sound of my words rising. I felt pathetic. I wondered what the fuck was wrong with me. I told Burn he couldn't do it. I was emotional. He

said it was already done and then nothing else. He was cold, frigid and icy, remorseless and dismissive.

I never saw it coming. Durban swung at me. His knuckle caught my lip and split it instantly, dazing me before I realized I was bleeding onto his shirt because he was driving through me, attacking me, forcing me to backpedal, trying to take me to the ground before stumbling momentum carried us through the window of World Duty Free. We landed amongst a shower of broken glass, into what must have been a display for men's cologne because I remember the smell, then fire in my eyes. Durban had taken a bottle of Hugo Boss and poured it across my face as if he were trying to blind me.

Burberry, not Hugo Boss. Of course I was trying to blind him. If me and Burn were about to have it out, I had seen enough to know I didn't stand a chance at fighting him straight. That fear made me strong, gifted a new power built and boiled from caverns in my body. I found myself in surprising control, forearm against his throat, driving through the back of his neck, disregarding, into the glass-splintered floor. Spit was falling from my mouth and onto his face. I could hear myself involuntarily hissing, watching veins bulge from his neck and from the side of his head. I was pressing so hard, the fight in his body left, desperate, begging for his sake, a man too proud, for me to relent. I screamed, urging him to take me on, to turn tables and deliver his famous pain. But he wasn't moving. Instead, he was just whimpering, trying to speak. I couldn't hear. I didn't give a fuck.

I loved Durban. In spite of everything he is and everything he had turned me into. Maybe that's why his despondence felt so betraying. Though I never expected what was happening, I understood it. I also understood that if I ever took on a fight, it would only serve to combat something I deemed evil in the world. That could never truly be him. I used to have dreams when I was growing up, fights with Michael, these vicious episodes that existed nothing like the way we existed in the real world. I don't know where they came from. We'd take turns smashing our hands into each other's faces, guard down, breaking bones until our faces appeared pulpy and unrecognizable. I'd wake and take days to get over repercussions of that, of make believe. Sometimes, I think maybe I never got over those visions, and how a person's good mind could betray them so terribly. I was looking up at John and saw my brother. He was more maniac and out of control than I would have ever been able to imagine. The sight of him gave me chills. He was taking my life, spitting all over me, then shaking before he composed and spoke clearly, "Remember how you fucked up tonight. Remember how unforgiving you were that I fucked up too, for being afraid and absent. Remember you had every right to leave me, and to go, but that tonight, I was here, and I was willing, and you saw it in my fucking eyes. You remember that, and that I forgave you."

At the height of things, he said, "Thank you." With that, an obvious weight seemed to spill from us. Then after another short breath he said, "Come on Johnny, quit breaking my heart." I think he said it like that to fuck with my sincerity, but also to reveal some of his own. He was suffocating, on the edge of going unconscious. I shot up and backed away, out the broken window, creating distance between us in case he came for me, as if it would have mattered. I guess I expected commotion in some form. Retaliation from Burn, detainment from airport security, or at the very least, someone to clean up the mess we'd made. There was nothing, not even an alarm. People were sleeping, stretched out across seats in nearby gates, who either ignored my screaming, or were unmoved by the sound that happens when a nearby ten by ten-foot glass window gets blown to fucking pieces by two stumbling madmen. Burn finally sat up, collected himself and his things. He was careful placing his hands around the

glass before getting up, before he stepped out to meet me, before he looked me in the eyes. He dropped his bag at my feet, spoke softly, "Alright Johnny, alright. Until the end. But you need to be better." He apologized when I agreed. Then I apologized for everything. He told me I had glass in my face and asked if he had any in his. I said no. That was a strange lie.

We found our way to gate sixteen, London to Chicago to Los Angeles. We found a seat on shitty stained carpeting, taking turns playing DJ. There were passengers around who were sleeping soundly before we decided to show up, who relocated one by one until the gate was empty. Burn said he was starting to feel settled, with his girl, with his work, with his past and future. He said things inside of him were beginning to steady, like he had finally adapted to the speed of the game. I couldn't relate to what he was talking about and hated myself for that. He said, "I'll play it for you," and without even thinking, put on "Trailer Trash." We sat there and listened, passed the bottle back and forth and I felt like I got it, because of the look he had in his eye, because Burn is so good at stuff like that. Bringing me along.

INSERT SKETCH: DURBAN AND BURN ON THE CARPET EMPTY TERMINAL – IPOD AND BOTTLE

We were in need of a new adventure, somewhere neither of us had been, that's what I told him. He said it was already in the works. Then he made me swear Michelle would come. We sat there a while, maybe another hour, talking through shuffling songs and tending wounds. "Cosmic Dancer" was the last thing I remember, John Durban singing T. Rex before I fell asleep.

I woke at 7:10 and there was a flight attendant standing over me, trying to say something I couldn't hear because Sinead O'Connor was singing full-blast, next to my head. I looked around. Durban was gone. Herculean, he had stacked at least six rows of chairs in front of the outlet powering the iPod dock so no one could unplug it, and wrapped at least two rolls of masking tape around the iPod and the dock to ensure nothing would be removed or interrupted. Then, he must have set the alarm. When the song ended, "Nothing Compares to You," it started again. That's what he left me with – Sinead on repeat and a note taped to my chest. It said exactly, "Like the fog of London, motherfucker."

RIO DE JANERO
December 31, 2008

Brazil was a mad house. Every inch of every sidewalk was full white, full of beautiful masses wandering and wild, already boisterous at barely three in the afternoon. I thought it wasn't like Durban to bring us to a place like Rio on a night like New Years. It seemed out of his character. He is, above everything and contrary to popular belief, discrete. As happy as I was to be there, to be with John again, and as happy as I was to feel the adrenaline of a new country with Michelle by my side, I found myself unable to let go of a suspicion, for whatever reason, that our entire rendezvous was going to become more than we could handle.

I must confess, there was a reason behind Rio. It wasn't just to celebrate the turning of a calendar year. Months ago, I hired a private investigator and put him on the payroll to find someone for me. I didn't tell Burn, couldn't tell Burn I was there for Jenny, didn't want him to think I wasn't present in every right for he and Michelle. I was going to be that too. This isn't justification and this isn't an apology. If ever I'm drifting, I think back to Berlin, to simplify – I'm dead tonight, every night until I am. Burn gave us that. Jenny still out there, alive and alone puts me in violation. When the time came where he would have to understand my actions, I knew he would. Because he is who he is, of the highest caliber. I told the P.I. that when he found her, the only information I wanted was the city. That was going to be my compromise. I believed that if the two of us occupied the same place for the same week, I would find her without looking, no matter the expanse. Nothing could stop that. I had been sick, fucking sick. Rio rescued me. It gave me new breath. That's all I could feel, walking the streets for five days before Burn and Michelle showed up, eighteen

hours a day with my eyes open, dreaming reunion, likely missing her by half-streets or steps at a time.

We pulled into gates that stood a throw from Ipanema. John had earlier said on the phone to not worry about the anarchy of Rio, that the place we were staying could remove us from it at any point. Once inside, I knew exactly what he meant. The hotel was called Amarasco and it was a fortress – armed guards, moats and majestic. The air in Rio had a sweetness I could taste, like sugar rode the breeze. We walked into the lobby and Durban was standing there. His smile warm. The moment he saw us, he came barreling in and wrapped me in a hard, tight hug. When he let loose, I slapped his face so hard, it shook him and the room. He laughed like a maniac, not feeling a thing. John turned to Michelle and introduced himself, agonizing over not paying her the attention she was due in Cape Town. Then, he apologized for not getting to her before I did, speaking in bursts of how it was regarded as one of the great travesties in his life. John is literally a new man every time I see him, re-invented. That's what I was thinking, and of how inspired I was to always witness it. A young waiter came out of nowhere to hand us three drinks, true caipirinhas. He traded them for our bags and that's how the night began. John raised his glass and spoke a toast, "Never a moment escape." I felt heavy then light, beyond the weight of the world and above all it took to deliver us there. In a span of moments, John erased any doubts I had about being anywhere but Rio.

It had only been a few months since I had last seen Burn, but things had changed between us. After the first drink, I led Burn into a promise. With Michelle as our witness, we would go no longer than a month without seeing each other. I was overly dramatic during the declaration and realized this when Burn fired a look about my not mentioning any other obligations we may or may not have enacted in the past. It was obvious Michelle didn't know, and that Burn wasn't ready for her to know. I nodded when she looked away.

Michelle and Burn went upstairs to change and left me alone. According to my source, Jenny was leaving on New Year's Day. In less than twenty-four hours, we would no longer be moving in and occupying the same city. I ordered another drink, took it down between breaths and let it settle things, for a moment, knowing the calm and trust I had found in South America was soon ending.

The three of us left on foot after watching the sun go down from the balcony, into the streets to let the rush of vibrant life bombard us. I bought a six-pack of Brahma from an apartment window, handed two to Burn and two to Michelle. My aim was to find the Cariocas, so that we could mingle with and impersonate them. Everyone, everywhere was moving to the beach. Naturally, I took us against the grain. I told Burn and Michelle we were going to let the jungle have us until midnight. At that time, we would return to the waterfront, to see the fireworks. Because in my heart that's what felt right...to celebrate life, our lives that remained, somehow knowing Jenny would be there, mixed somewhere in the mass of a crowd so large it could make her disappear.

We walked for miles, stopping at four or five Brazilian dives until things thinned out enough for us to hail a cab. Durban then handled everything, taking us into rainforest, at least the fringe of it. He stopped the cab in the middle of nowhere, then handed over enough cash to retain the driver for the night. There was a hostess and torches and she said something Durban relayed as, "Go on ahead, it isn't far." I wasn't sure what "it" was and Durban certainly wasn't about to tell me before we were walking through the damp and dark. I was hearing creature noises I'd never heard and everything I smelled felt new and invigorating. All we had to follow was a line of mismatched torches, walking for a good five minutes before I heard Samba, seven before we came to it – what Durban called a Carioca speakeasy. Whatever it was, it was magnificent, a stone bowl restaurant carved into the side of a rock cliff, with waterfalls and currents rushing all around our backs and feet, over our heads. Voices and sounds were bouncing off the rocks, reaching out into the night, pulling us in. The world surrounding us was so moving and alive, I remember thinking Durban had slipped something into our drinks, as if there had to be explanation or cause behind every great force I experienced in life. When I asked him, he laughed and said, "I know, right?"

Our table was tucked away in the far corner and had been reserved. The maître d' initially summoned John, holding four fingers up on his hand. John tried to nonchalantly and promptly shake him off. That was the first sign. The place was full, and to reach our table, we had to navigate tight passages and cross every face. Every one of them seemed to be studying our approach. At first it made me uncomfortable to think we were taking the last table of someone's friend or neighbor, someone who belonged there and would have otherwise come to escape people like us. But it wasn't like that. In fact, the faces I was projecting upon began to do everything in their power to expel my discomfort with smiles and kisses and handshakes, like they had sensed and wanted to destroy my fear. The beauty in Brazil is no myth, and its people are the definition – dark and tanned skin, piercing eyes, tight and fierce bodies. They are pure vitality. Life in Rio comes bursting with a slow and mysterious grace. I could feel it building as we walked through the room, as at least one member of each table, table after table raised a glass to greet us, to pay welcome, saying something unclear I think only locals said to one another – that we then began repeating back to them, to anyone, to everyone. Our waiter dropped a porcelain jug onto the center of our table as we sat. I asked Durban what it was and he said he wasn't sure, but that if he had to guess after tasting – softened Brazilian moonshine. It was sweeter than I expected it to be. Durban told us we could drink it all night and be alright, an authority on belligerence, saying exactly, "It'll wreck us but not destroy us."

From the moment we sat, waiters began offering churrasco for the table. Samba was rolling and couples were dancing. The night was already marvelous and unfolding. I looked to John but he was looking off, somewhere into the black of jungle outside. The more time we spent with him, the more obvious it became – John was withholding. He began checking his phone and tapping his hands and feet, everything in a patter. When he became remotely still, we talked about his roaming life and of ours in Los Angeles. I told him we had bought a small place on Coldwater and moved in together. He nearly choked. Then, he leaned in and kissed our cheeks, wiped some form of tear from his eye. No matter what was going on with him, I can say one thing for sure about that night and every night I've ever spent with John – when he is happy, it is the most genuine thing. He was happy for Michelle and I, kept saying it over and over, that and how great it was to have both of us there with him. It meant the world. Those were his words. Still, something was off. There were several points where Michelle and I would be talking or watching the band and I'd turn to see John had escaped outside, pacing in the darkness, fighting for a phone signal he would never find. I tried not to think too much of it, knowing John preferred my level of concern remain low, so that's what I set out to do, be distantly there for him. When we were alone, I turned to Michelle and watched her as she watched the band. She was starting to get stars in her eyes, we all were. I found her hand beneath the table in the midst of one of Durban's absences. She leaned across the table and kissed me perfectly.

Fuck, I'd been careless. Time was running out and I had barely even taken a minute to think of that as a possibility, not finding Jenny, not setting things right. Leaving without her began to creep my thoughts, aware that I could have known exactly where she was at any moment in Rio. I hired people to give me that power

only to refuse it. The three of us started to fall under the spell of the drinks, and after dinner, I began to slip away, continuously telling Burn and Michelle I was lining things up for the night. I think we were all deep enough that no one suspected anything. There were a couple stretches of time where I stayed away, outside the restaurant, just to watch them. They were so beautiful together. I watched as she wooed and pulled him up to dance, as they shuffled and turned their feet on that dim wooden floor, beneath the diamond star sky. I felt tenderness that wouldn't long before have been mistaken for weakness. I stood there thinking of how he had found it, the thing he had always been looking for, his Girl. Maybe I'm too selfish a person to sit back and enjoy that, to be a witness and so simply remain content. I wanted it for myself, my Girl, and she was close, in Rio and obviously so was I. I couldn't let go. It was a quarter past ten and I was breaking down somewhere in the middle of a jungle, playing false cool, pretending life and every fucking thing would just work itself out, trusting like a goddamned fool in a device so corrupt as fate.

Durban was still gone, somewhere outside. I went out to check up on him and he waved me off, faking like he was on some call when I knew he wasn't. From a distance, he looked like a child left behind, hand raised in the air and waiting for another hand to return. There was only one thing in the world capable of doing that to him. I had seen a flash of it in London, at the bar in Heathrow but this was different. This time, it was local. Jenny was there, somewhere in Rio. Durban had ulterior motives.

Michelle was waiting for me on the floor beside the band. There were six of them, probably anywhere from twenty to fifty years old. All night, I watched as the drink girls filled their glasses and ours, passing us all into a composed drunk. There have been times lately when I thought I had it all figured out — that my grip on life and how it should be played was as good as any living thing. But I had a moment right then, watching the band play and dreaming up the fairytale lives I wished upon them to have, where I knew nothing and wanted to be exactly what they were, to erase what I'd done in Berlin and live past one hundred years, pushing on days until the world grew tired of me. Taking in Rio made me realize how short our time was, and that I had two years left to discover the extent of everything. Durban was being evasive again, and until he corrected himself, I didn't care that he was outside and hurting. I knew we would be a part of his story, however his story was going to play out that night – and that we would absolutely be there for him, no matter what that meant, because Durban's well-being means everything to me. But also, fuck him. In that moment, it wasn't my place to be anywhere but where I was, holding onto Michelle, letting Brazilian flow soak our bodies. Whatever was coming for us that night was coming, I could feel it. I was ready for it.

Durban came back inside. I watched as he grabbed our waiter and settled up. He made a seat for himself on top of the closest table and watched us. Michelle and I were slowly turning when I faced him. It looked like he was forcing calm over his body, forcing patience, following our movement with his eyes. When I turned away from John and Michelle turned to face him, she asked me why he was the way he was. I didn't have time to answer. She stopped turning, pulled away and looked right at me, as if she knew I was keeping something important from her. She felt that, but let it go. A time will come. That's what I told myself as the three of us waited for the song to finish, and then left, hearts set on Ipanema and meeting the New Year.

We split from the cab one mile from the beach, fifty-seven minutes until midnight. I told them everything on the ride back because Burn said, "Stop fucking lying to me Durban." I talked about the time I spent with her father, not the first time, but of my three subsequent visits to Amalfi, and the hopes I had of forcefully

reuniting with her. I talked about the men I hired to find her, and the information they had given. In hearing myself speak these things aloud, I felt very pathetic. No one owes anything to anyone in this world and I know that, knew it as I was saying it and long before Jenny showed up in my life. When I stopped talking, Michelle moved in close and let me hug her. Things hurt all over and I think I cried a little bit but it was dark enough that no one saw.

Somehow, we cut our way through about a million people and reached the waterfront. It was eighteen minutes to midnight and everything was constricting. We could see the gate to our hotel a few blocks down the road but there was no way we were going to make it. Burn could see me still pressing and said, "Stop Johnny. Try and see this world." I couldn't. I couldn't see anything, or feel anything but need. Only she could resolve it. I could see the pity in his eyes, the confirmation that Rio and my turmoil and his bliss had collectively pronounced our endeavors on pace. He took my phone and sent a text to my source, almost instantly finding out for himself, exactly where she was staying. He grabbed a hold of my face with two hands, crushing it to tell me in an elevated whisper that we would go see her in the morning, when things calmed down, when we had heads clear enough to figure out how to handle her. He said he would help me. The word help was echoing in my mind when something happened – a chime rang through my body and my throat turned dry. I became dizzy, like I had been poisoned. The sea of white and surrounding bodies began to shift violently towards us, dividing us. I could hear Michelle calling my name but I was being pushed away. Her calls were fading. I was alone. There became a split in the crowd, as a path formed its way to a single body, alone in the middle of everything. It was then I stopped believing in life and existence and reality as actual things. There were millions in Rio, millions, and as she turned and I saw those eyes, I thought I was dead already, uncertain I could ever survive in a world where magic like that existed. It was Jenny, in Rio, standing before me for the first time since the day she left.

I lifted Michelle onto my shoulders so we wouldn't lose him. We were both barely moving, searching through cracks in the crowd as she called out. There was no way we could get to him. I saw Durban the instant his soul left his body. I followed his gaze through the opening in the crowd – the crowd that had suddenly and impossibly split and parted in front of him. For miles, there was so little room to move, the three of us had to hold hands just to stay together, claustrophobic before space appeared, before she appeared – John's walking fire. It was a movie, or myth or fable. Then she turned and saw him. A line was created between their gaze so heated, so dangerous, it repelled the crowd, as if trespassing between Durban and his Jenny could slice a person through. I've talked about time standing still in my past and immediately began to fear for the falseness of it all, realizing I could not have spoken truth until that moment, until I had actually seen the world stop.

INSERT SKETCH: JENNY IN THE MIDDLE OF MILLIONS – THE CROWD REPELLED – FIREWORKS

Her hair was cut, like it had been pulled out. She didn't move and wasn't moving. She was gone. People were moving away from her. There was a sudden explosion over the water, then another. Soon, hundreds of explosions broke the sky, rocketing light upon the shore. I turned to Burn and asked him if what I was seeing was real. But it wasn't Burn. It was a strange man, and he didn't understand me. I stepped towards Jenny and she stood her ground, without expression, waiting. I felt my heart melting and clogging my veins. I could taste it. I could taste my broken, melting heart. I wanted to scream her name, to hold her so tight her bones shattered and collapsed. I took another step.

We stood back, watching them, fighting the swaying crowd. I thought Jenny would move to him, or acknowledge him but she didn't, or wasn't about to. When I realized this, the appearance of the world began to bend around us. Michelle clenched my hand so hard. The immediate air turned stale. Everywhere, there was happiness and celebration but all I could feel was an approaching void, exactly as Durban had described. Even from a distance. John explained her power as one to remove and create a world where only they existed. It took Rio to understand. He closed in; close enough to kneel, which he did. She must have finally recognized who he was.

I reached out to touch her hand and she let me. She placed her other hand on the side of my face and held it gently. I wanted to weep but couldn't, because I couldn't let her see that. Not then. She knelt, to the ground to meet me, to look into me, to give us one last moment together, one last moment I would forever try to live inside. Then she began screaming. Strangers moved in and pulled me away from her. Fucking heroes. I fought them, flailing, giving and taking punches. Burn's voice was raging in the background, calling for me, to get to me, to defend me. When I looked up, Jenny was drifting away, into the crowd. I kept her eyes for as long as I could, calling her name. Begging.

Cheers circled from every direction, from the faces of a million strangers lit in abundance of color and hope and love, wooed by the sky's parade of light and sound. They had no idea worlds beside them were crumbling. I could hear John calling out to her as he fought off attack, as she came around a wave of revelers and stopped right beside me. Her eyes explained every contradiction Durban had ever painted.

Durban saw us together and screamed for me to stop her. On instinct, I reached out and held her arm. She said nothing. I told her I was going to take him away forever, and that he loved her more than he ever loved anything. She looked through me. When I let go, she looked back to Durban one last time. She blew him a kiss before the crowd swallowed her whole. I worried he'd never forgive me.

I found Michelle and took her hand but it wasn't enough. I had to kiss her and hold her before we could even think about helping John. We stood there together, in immense moments that lasted forever. I gathered myself. I made sure she was okay, and that she was still mine. When we reached Durban, he was alone and unsteady. He called my name before his eyes fell shut and he tumbled into my grasp. Michelle took his other side and our fear began anew as we struggled to hold him up. The fireworks were on crescendo when I thought I saw Jenny again like a ghost in the crowd, watching Durban. Several explosions lit her face enough to reveal tears but I couldn't understand what they meant. Not before she was gone.

Michelle and I were dragging John's full weight. He was hardly breathing and I became hysterical, screaming for the crowd to clear. Somehow and suddenly, a team of EMT's helped open a path to their parked ambulance. Without explanation, we were in the back of it and then moving away. John was on a gurney and I thought at any moment, they were going to tell us he would be fine, that there was nothing really wrong with him. That never happened. They gave him oxygen and put an IV into his arm. I remember a distinct look of dismay or confusion on the faces of the paramedics, and began to fear the possibility that John could die of a broken heart.

<h1 style="text-align:center"><u>EDITOR'S NOTE</u></h1>

The following is a transcribed letter found folded in the back pocket of the manuscript binder. It was written by Romero, a 24-year-old sailor located in Italy on the island of Capri. The letter was tucked inside an envelope, which was also included, and was shipped overnight express to an address in London, the home of John Durban. It was dated May 13, 2009.

John,

It has been some time. I saw her after she left you. After you came back. Wherever we went and whatever we did, she always found a way to your name. Please know you did not just pass. She was made different. I like to believe if you find what you found with her, you have lived in this life. Believe that now.

She has gone John. I found her this morning. If there were something more than words, or better I could give, I would. There is nothing.

Your friend always,

Rome

TOKYO
June 17, 2009

I was flying from London to Tokyo because I'd never been. There was something inside me under the impression that I had to see and feel and consume the lights and people of a country defined by chaotic perceptions in my mind. I must've fallen asleep because I was having a dream about her. She'd been meeting me in my sleep, the positive or negative result of which would have complete control over my state upon waking. If it was me and her and we were anything remotely close to good, I'd wake up functional, thinking she wasn't so far away, thinking it was possible she'd somehow soon return. Flip side, if I dreamt about the life she was incapable of keeping, or of what had happened to her, I'd wake pumping poison, looking to spit blood and venom in the faces of any fuckers who came near me. This particular dream fell into an evolved, combined category. It began where we began, on the beach in St. Tropez, alone, not another body in sight. I remember feeling the power of her beside me, believing she was still alive and that the pictures of her death, of her cut throat, of her blood covering a white floor and her pale, naked body that I demanded to see because it's what I was owed, because she was mine and mine alone, was the dream. When I woke and reality took hold, I can state with authority that no living thing could have handled such an arriving moment with grace. Her death was my fault. People who care about my well-being will fight this theory until the end. But the fact remains. If I stayed away she wouldn't have done that to herself. She wouldn't have died so horribly, and alone.

Turbulence had brought me back and everything was wrong, so fucking wrong. The engines were humming and I could feel the suffocating assholes all around me, surrounding me. They were caving my world. I remember the fasten seatbelt sign and needing to stand like it was my only savior, so I stood. I remember needing to scream like it was my only savior, so I screamed until I tasted blood, needing to be anything but still or seated or silent. I remember fear and panic flooding the other passengers' eyes, especially the eyes of the children. I remember stepping outside of myself, out of body, watching from above, my life and the pieces it had fragmented into. There was a struggle and then a bump to the top of my head. Dark heat began running down my face. A woman screamed then fainted and that's one of the last things I recall, before I was driven into the ground, before my hands were pinned behind my back, before I felt a pinch and a cool burn running through my veins, before I saw the eyes of a pitying and stout and balding Asian man who was peeking in from coach. I wanted it all to be over. He knew.

I woke up jailed and asked the guard where. He said Arakawa, just outside midtown Tokyo. My head was beating like it had its own heart, a feeling explained by the seventeen stitches holding tight the slice of life resting ten inches above my right eye. Once I was awake and coherent, I was brought into a questioning room where both sides, mine and the airline's, agreed to part amicably…at least without filing any charges. One of the male stewards had struck me in the head with an undisclosed blunt object. That much they offered. I will offer that I was having a psychotic episode in a concealed space 25,000 feet above the ground. Still, they showed poor restraint, and knew this. The airline, which I cannot legally mention – but I can't keep anyone from narrowing the field based on my itinerary, has done a decent job keeping the entire incident under wraps. Sometimes I Google, "Man Goes Berserk On Airplane From London To Tokyo" and a story appears.

There was amateur footage on YouTube for a day before it was taken down. When I type the search in CAPS, I always have better luck. That was two weeks ago. As if any of this matters.

People tell me I live an eventful life. In the past, at a point, maybe that would have made everything worthwhile. I don't know. Truth is I don't know what I am anymore. I'm just floating now and that's not what I want to be. I came to Tokyo to get out of London, to let the speed culture consume me. I've spent the last ten days inside some obscure hotel, in bed, sleeping on and off, watching Japanese television or sitting in the dark and quiet, wasting away, coming to terms with where I have been and where I have come from. I was told about a small service for her that I didn't attend for a thousand reasons. Not a single one was valid. Without me there, words were spoken and her ashes were let go into the Mediterranean. Still, she won't depart.

AMALFI
June 23, 2009

I can't stop thinking of what she was thinking at the end, when she knew her end was coming…when it was close. She used to speak about slowing the world, this fantasy of paralyzing our time together so that nothing could touch or divide us. Control. I'm thinking about the moments when her last semblance of it faded away. Maybe she succeeded, right then, and found that pause…sometime on or around her last breath. I wonder if I crossed her mind. I wonder if she thought of herself as the girl who left me behind – the one who had what it took to stand me on my feet and keep me there. I'm thinking of her blood stretching across that perfect white floor and all I want to know, the only thing I want to know was whether or not she thought of me. Because I'm selfish, and a motherfucker, and I deserve to know. I'd give everything I have for that.

There is a place I feel like we first became, between the wall where I wrecked her Alfa Romeo and the ledge where they let her ashes go. It's a grass cove, a perch tucked below the highest point on the Amalfi coastline. We'd bring a blanket and rope and risk our lives for the paradise of that Italian sunset, spending our days and nights making love to the violent waters below. We'd talk about everything she'd allow, slowly turning each other inside out. There is still so much I never knew. That's what I was always thinking. That's what I was thinking when I returned, alone, to the cold wind pleading stay away.

There was a crack in the wall of that perch only we knew about. It was about ten feet off the ground, only accessible with a small climb or boost or dangling jump. Inside of it, there was room for us to stash whatever we saw fit – matches, keys, mementos. I hadn't been back since the last time we slept the night there together, as happy as two people with our dealings could have been. It was perfect. I understand the appearance of my using that word on her, and on us.

In dreams, I had been seeing the crack often. There, it's a cavern — scary and infinite. I am meant to enter. Outside, the world I must leave behind is the opposite — safe and defined. My path is never conflicted. I hear her voice calling and become helpless to follow, thinking I can help her, thinking I can design new rules on life and death, and find her, take her hand, bring her back to the real world, where I can tell her how terribly I need her, repair her, repair myself. I understand the appearance of these confessions. I can feel my heart smashing against bone. Violent revolt. Even when I sleep, I can feel my eyes pouring, tears falling off my face and onto some real world pillow or floor. It's fucked. This is the battle of my life. I am not detached.

I stepped onto a ledge and reached inside the crack. We had left behind an old and rusted flask that was her father's, and still smelled like cheap grappa. There was a ring, silver and black. I bought it for Jenny from some gypsy on a bridge in Florence but she never saw it. I can't explain why. The crack was damp and empty and I was losing balance one moment before I found and held her last offensive. Like forcing my hand down, through the tip of a diseased icy blade, I immediately felt a letter, a postcard. Holding it, the last remaining bits of her spirit or will arrived and began surging my body, seeking out anything that remained intact, living, hopeful, to rip those things apart. In that moment I understood, Jenny was giving me something I could never understand — that her clearance and the pain forged into every thought I had of her, thousands per passing minute, could only be put to rest once she had destroyed me fully. Sweet Jenny. The letter was her gift. I held it in my hand, unable to breathe before I could, my eyes slow dancing her last words to the world.

The waves were crashing below me. Burn's text flashed across my phone, "Miss you. More than a month." I closed my eyes, imagined her ashes still floating beside me, in the air, as if parts of her had been, and would have always been waiting for my return. I imagined her falling onto my face and arms, soaking through my skin. I imagined her in my blood, flowing through my veins and into my heart, calming and quieting it, speaking in a whisper, "Everything will now be alright." For a moment at least, I felt corrected, being there, paying out my eyes to the coast we owned together. I looked over the edge of the cliff and gave it thought, for a moment at least, of how easy it would be to take that step. Sometimes, I wish it were in me. But it's not. I'm not Jenny. I'm not here to clear up any misconceptions about her. The girl was fucked. I don't know what that made or makes me, but it makes me something. When I close my eyes, I will always see her face, the singular truth of everything she was. I will never know another.

LOS ANGELES
October 18, 2009

I recently extended an invitation for John to come and stay with us in Los Angeles for as long as he wanted. I thought that with everything he had been through, it would be good for everyone. Plus, I always miss my friend and was worried about him. When Jenny died, I flew to London to take him to the service but he couldn't do it. So instead, the two of us spent the week at his apartment. He wasn't eating much, or saying much. In the middle of most nights, he would leave to go on a long walk. At first, I worried he would never come back. One night I followed him to the River Thames at 2 AM. He stood by the guardrail without moving, looking out at the water until dawn. Then he walked home. He maybe mentioned her name twice that week, even as I made a constant effort to get him talking. He only said, "Please don't."

After I left him in London and got back home, he started sending me cryptic e-mails, or texts, or he would call at odd times and then hang up without saying a word. Messages left were fragmented at best. He was certain someone was stalking him, and spoke of waking up in the middle of the night to find dark figures standing at the foot of his bed. I didn't hear anything for a while before he sent word from Kathmandu. I couldn't imagine what he was doing there. Michelle and I were both afraid for him.

NEW DELHI
November 2, 2009

Before the sun comes up, Delhi sits in purgatory. There's an invading stench even before the heat begins that's primed to erupt. I was standing somewhere that had a view of the stars, thinking out loud in the middle of the night, probably on the roof of my hotel in Old Delhi, and the smell was beginning to move in, taking hold of my senses, pulling out the few confronting forces still left existing in me and delivering them to a plane in front of my face. I need to personify the smell to do it justice, to demonstrate how relentless it was, how it kept saying over and over, "Here, you fuck. Feel me now."

I was on the street, running because that's what Burn taught me to do, to help myself. I headed out looking for a park, a big block of green I had seen on a map, thinking I could make it there by memory before getting lost, before happening upon this Shahi mosque that appeared abandoned. There was a park to its left, a triangular path orbiting splotches of dead grass in the center. Inside of the path was a graveyard of squat toilets, rows upon rows, what must have been sixty of them, placed into the ground and lining my northern lap. In the center of the park, a German Shepherd was chained to one of the toilets, barking, choking itself in hopes that it might break free and tear me apart, tracing my progress the entire time, ferocious, navigating its allotted circumference, grinding metal against rusted metal as it pulled and fought. Indians sleeping across the ground didn't stir. I figured every six laps would equal a mile, and decided I was going to run until I felt better. Clearer. Ten laps in, the sun was rising. The city was waking. On the east side of the path, people began to watch me from the street while waiting for buses, standing within feet of my passing. At thirty laps, some of them began to spit at my feet.

The dog would not let up. I suppose I wouldn't either. Prisoner. Neither would the crowd. At fifty laps, there were nearly two lines of people at the fence. Their spitting had progressed to my eyes and face. It was a game by then, to run through their assault. Grace made them incendiary. At seventy, the spitters had thinned and were replaced by a kind father and his sweet daughter. The young girl handed me an Indian Gatorade called Pocari Sweat, already open, half-full that tasted like sweet grapefruit. By then, Delhi was an inferno. At eighty, a pack of evil dogs turned up to attack the chained German Shepherd, whom I defended then befriended, before setting free. At ninety, the fence was lined with schoolchildren in uniform. Some of them would cheer as I passed. At ninety-nine, I stopped running, and walked away.

...

Life is a cell filling with shit. A floor, four walls, and an open ceiling. From the moment I was born, shit came pouring in, putrid and heavy, telling me to give up, submerge, choke. Give in once, find that floor and it's likely you'll likely never get up. Because there's comfort there. Because at least the floor is something to stand on. Because at least one exists in the company of billions, who have all convinced themselves of worse places to be, of worse things to do. But accept that floor, normalize it, and no peace will ever arrive. So, a decision has to be made. Spend the rest of life letting shit compound over you, or fight out. Every day, survive the day. We don't sink because we're weak, we sink because we stop believing in escape above. And because everything, everywhere, seems designed to pull us under, to keep us there. Even beside all I was born into, make no mistake, I was still born on that floor. I could not buy, or fuck, or use my way up. I tried. My whole life. There are reasons I love Burn as much as I do. But one in particular. Until he came, I never fought for a thing.

The following written correspondence was sent from an address in New York to John Durban in London. It was included inside of the original manuscript's binder, and has been transcribed.

John,

I received your letter. My business manager said she hadn't heard from you in a while. I took you in a gutter. Now this. You reject the trust. I can only imagine how sobering it's going to be to learn that you have successfully severed yourself.

With your signature and declarations, both received, my lawyers have determined your desires legally binding. As of this letter's mailing you hold no stake in my company, business or otherwise. I thought I'd give you 30 years in this world to understand how the world works. The last thing I ever wanted was a child, you John, barely edging out your unholy mother. What a fairytale.

Good luck my boy. In the immortal words of so many of the eternally compassionate that have preceded, you are dead to me. But let us be honest, you've always known that.

James Durban
12-9-09

COLOMBO TO MATARA
January 24, 2010

I was exhausted, hanging by threads, standing on platform #5 in Colombo. "Welcome to the Machine" was playing in my ears, somehow appropriate, swaying me because of stillness, not weakness, back and forth, waiting for a train to come and take me away. South. Track #6 came in. Masses spilled. I was bumped hard by some kid and felt a release around my leg. The strap to my bag had been unhooked and was on the ground. Theft. I had just missed it. Of course, everything was inside – my clothes, computer, passport, sparse words on India, Jenny's letter. There were so many people around me, so many bags everywhere, I had already forgotten what mine looked like...so much movement. There wasn't even a place to begin. That's when I saw him, this teenage kid already accepting my defeat, thirty meters ahead. He turned, wearing a red and white shirt, fucked because he looked right at me. Because he had stolen the only pertinent things I had left in the world.

We both took off. I heard a whistle three times, sharp and echoing against the ceilings and walls of that cavern station. I thought it was the police, thought it was someone helping me. The noise was just ahead, a beacon, ringing again and again and again. It wasn't help, but the kid blowing a signal, step one when he's been spotted and a chase begins. They must have caught me on the way in, the way I carry myself. Not long ago, I would have been a dream mark, the kind petty thieves look back on and talk about for the rest of their careers, at least ten thousand in cash on my person at all times. Of course, not long ago, I would have never been in Sri Lanka. Across the platforms and overpasses, the frantic station became somewhat calm. There were no trains leaving, no trains coming. Any commotion within became glaring and apparent. I could see more of these kids approaching, swarming ahead and in my peripherals. They were changing their shirts to red and white, already all wearing the same dark and matching pants, all with the same build, recruited for duplicity. I understood things didn't usually come to what we came to, a mistake on their part. Certainly they were usually stealth, never realized until long gone.

I had been yelling things, screaming generic things like stop that motherfucker he's got my bag, but everyone just moved aside, slipped back, like they knew better than to interfere. It didn't surprise me. I'm not sure I would have helped me either, and almost respected them more because of that. The kid wasn't far ahead when a different kid passed, bumped him and exchanged my bag for another one. The different kid was running at me then, steps from me when I lowered my shoulder, full speed, before we collided. I felt his body collapse around me, coupled with some internal pop that had to have been a diaphragm, before he flew through the side window of a waiting train. My bag fell to the ground, which of course wasn't mine but a shitty replica, false exchange designed to give the outfit an extra sixty seconds of space, the time it took most of their targets, if lucky, to stop the decoy, search him with failure and then plead their case to some local authority. It didn't take me more than a few seconds before I was back in pursuit, thinking about the satisfaction that came from sending a fucking cog airborne.

I climbed a main overpass and stood above the twelve tracks, thinking I had lost him. What I saw was magnificent. In every row, two kids, boys like mine, were circling the length of each platform, running laps, all decoys. I marveled. Beside track #5, I could see the cog hobbling away, hunched and in terrible pain. No one was helping him. That didn't surprise me either. I screamed, defeated, smashed my forearm through a fiberglass fence, thinking of that first boy's face, occupied and dominated by a certain rage. That's when I saw him from a distance, clear as day and making a calm move for the exit. There, he would be out in the world, and unguarded. I took off my long-sleeve shirt and gave it to a beggar. There was a guy coming towards me wearing a green foam hat. I pulled it from his head for 10 USD's and headed for the exit, quite cool.

On the street, I picked him up and began to follow, walking quickly, on my toes, waiting for his break. I was drawing him in. He kept turning to look back, even into my eyes at one point, but never recognized me. In my mind, I had been playing out hopes for a daring chase through the streets of Colombo but the chances of that were quickly fading. He turned right, off the main road and towards an underpass. I was drawing closer, closer, on his heels before I reached my hand around his throat and pressed him into a choke against a crumbling concrete wall. He looked right at me and hardly flinched, hardly fearful, fifteen or sixteen at best. He was cocky, just smiling before, "What? What, America?" I was going to push into his eyeballs, to plunge into them with the tips of my fingers and pull. But I didn't. I bent my elbow, to put my sharpest bone through the side of his head. But I didn't. He was still smiling, very faintly, almost tragically. Then I knew why. Behind us, I could feel others circling, spotters who must have tailed me when I tailed him. He looked over my shoulder to three separate things, his militia. One of them said something in Sinhalese and we all waited. They were asking for orders. He took a couple beats before he looked to me, softly, before he looked back and spoke back, softly, disarming them. The air thinned. I looked to the bag on his shoulder. It only looked like mine. Mine was long gone. I eased my grip as a tear fell from my face. They slipped away.

When I got back to platform #5, the train still hadn't come. Somewhere in India, a woman said, "Things here are broken." The train eventually rolled in around five. I boarded with the clothes on my back, nearly empty pockets and a new green hat, finally on my way. We rolled out. Cash was low but the place I was staying was already taken care of.

We were moving past the outskirts of the city before we turned, before the buildings stopped and I realized the train was going to roll beside the ocean until the end of the line, all the way south. The sun was fading over a tropical, beautiful, devastated land. Mist from crashing salt water was coming in through the open windows. I was trying to lock memorable moments inside, to capture them tightly when a bag fell hard against the seat beside me. He was standing over it, my boy. He said, "They took what they wanted, money computer. Rest I didn't say. Passport there." I said nothing and opened the bag. Jenny's letter was still inside. He started to walk away before I grabbed him, too hard because he raised guard. I asked him to sit. He was reluctant at first, but then accepted. I asked how far he was going. He said Matara, end of the line. I told him I was going to Matara too, then Weligama, then Taprobane.

The boy introduced himself as Sadun and asked what I was doing in Sri Lanka, accusatory, like foreigners had no business there. I told him I was meeting someone. His eyes reminded me of Jenny's, of the space beneath them. I became obsessed with him then, pointing to and making reference to his eyes. I asked what made him the way he was. Sad. He was hesitant at first, refusing, which I couldn't accept. He said Sri Lanka was poor, but that wasn't it. He said Sri Lanka had been fighting forever, at war forever but that wasn't it. Then he said, "The wave," and our tone changed. We passed a blue sign at a crossing on the side of the road. There was a picture of a person and a tsunami chasing them with arrows pointing away from the ocean. He used it to help him speak again, "My sisters…"

They were riding the train home from Colombo in 2004, December 26, 9 AM when the wave hit. The cars were thrown off track, turning and flooding. Out of the fifteen-hundred riders, one thousand died, and three were his. He said the water flooded the open windows, "The hands of the waves" somehow closing them in, trapping all. He kept fighting forward, reaching out to his youngest sister until his mind went black and his body appeared in dirt, breathing air, alive, but alone. He found his middle sister first. He fell beside her and felt her soul, "With God." His oldest was "Broken in two," something I could not imagine. The youngest was still alive. Sadun knelt and took her hand. She was coughing blood, in pain, her torso purple and crushed. Sadun said, "She was suffering. I stayed with her. Until God took her. Many were lost that day. But it wasn't just them."

Sadun and I rode for hours to Matara, got out, and shook hands. He smiled and wished me luck with the friend I told him I was meeting on Taprobane, then said exactly, "I am sorry for taking your bag. If I could take wickets like Murali, I would not have to." I watched him wander a while, then disappear into darkness, past the faint light of a night market vendor.

There was a contact waiting to take me from Matara to Taprobane. He came up right away, tall and slender, very calm and somewhat inhospitable. He reached out his hand and introduced himself, "Bandula, minister and keeper of Taprobane Island." I realized then that everyone in Sri Lanka was like Sadun in some way, and that the tragedy of Sri Lanka ran the breadth of an entire country. Bandula motioned to a waiting Jeep, mentioned a welcome dinner and staff of five,

"Awaiting my arrival with great anticipation." We rode in silence along the coast for some miles. There was no music, no radio, only the roaring ocean. I could feel strength in the land, aggression from the moment I set foot in the country. We pulled over. Bandula parked the car on the side of the road and pointed out to sea, to torches one hundred meters away. It was Taprobane. I had seen pictures online in daylight, an island house unto itself, sitting on a rock in the ocean at the bottom of Sri Lanka, last land before Antarctica. He said the tide was low enough for me to walk, and that he would later follow. I got out of the car and moved across the sand and beach, through the shallow current and towards a lit, ivory entrance. Wading out, I felt a threshold against my body, as if some force was trying to impede my arrival. I had to push through, until the air became fragrant and alive. I stepped out of the water, onto the wooden dock of Taprobane, and approached the house, the place Alexandr had mentioned in Berlin, where his ancestors were killed, four years after an order was placed on their lives. This was the place Alexandr agreed to meet me, three years and one month after he claimed to have placed orders on the lives of myself and Burn. It was time to know the truth.

The following passages were taken from John Durban's freehand journal while on Taprobane Island. They have been transcribed without edit.

Alex showed up. Came alone. I came to this place with so much hope. No more. Berlin was not a bluff. Alex paid 2 million. Accounts were settled. Burn should not have touched the phone.

For two days, I have pleaded. For anything resembling a way out. I gave myself to him. In every way he wanted. Met every desire. It was not false. Before he left, he said, "If there is a way, I will find it and bring it to you. You have changed. I'm sorry."

There are mirrors everywhere here. Reflections everywhere. The biggest stood in the front hall, ten foot tall, four wide. Past tense. I woke up at sunrise. Found it shattered, one thousand pieces across the floor. Bandula appeared, spoke of my walking again in sleep, a spirit inside, stopped in front of the mirror to talk, to my reflection, casually, defiantly, eyes half open, face pressing the glass. Because of prior actions, he determined I broke the mirror in the middle of the night. Said when anyone was around to witness my behavior, that I was to be shaken awake and guided back to one of the rooms. Tucked into bed. Like a child. I asked why he never mentioned anything before. He said I had already demanded to be left alone on so many occasions, the staff wanted to avoid me altogether. "Are you certain you are of sound mind, Mister Durban?" Not the first time I have been asked. Wants me to be checked out and far away. Leave and not come back. Forfeit. I am not welcome. All would be better served by my departure. But I can't leave yet. There is magic here. I have seen her. Never let Burn see this.

January 30, 2010

Staff resigned today. "Concerns of safety beside Mr. Durban." They left a note without goodbye. Bandula read the note aloud before he came to a word I didn't understand. When I asked what it meant he said, "Devil." Corrected with, "Business in Trincomalee." He says it's a town up the eastern coast. I asked Bandula if he will also leave. He said it wouldn't be fitting. The staff could not afford to lose my commissions. He asked who I thought I'd been talking to, out there, by the ocean. I walked away. Told him his English fucking sucks. Too difficult to understand. Not true.

January 31, 2010

Rain disturbs the water in the pool. She is walking back and forth on the far side. By the ocean. So beautiful. I'll watch forever.

The ocean black. I don't understand how any Sri Lankan could go into it again — betrayed so terribly. Took so much. How can they build their homes next to it again? Along every mile of the coast. Or ever turn their backs on it again? Rest beside it. Its cold heart always beating. They can't escape. I am looking at the ocean. It is looking back, through me, speaking to me. Agony.

February 1, 2010

Sleep has left me. I walk to the coastline. Run for hours. Mainland people call me names Bandula won't translate. I dream without sleep. The waves return. I hear them and run, never fast enough. All is swallowed. Or, there are cobras in my bed. Mainlanders used to dump them here. They strike, I fall, hit the cold floor. Hard. Sometimes I stay for hours. Afraid to move. Sometimes cobras cover the grounds and I am trapped. Or they are the ocean and I am trapped. Or 30,000 dead are the ocean, floating, and I am trapped. The sun is setting.

Told Bandula about Jenny. He apologized for what she did then, "It is a problem in Sri Lanka. Young take their lives." He said, "Some cannot understand there is life beyond that which happened. I fear you are one of them." I chased him down. He drove me away, violent. Called me sick. Obsessed. Said, "You keep asking about death that came here. That is why they leave. Call you devil. We did not seek answers. Who are you? Peace you are looking for, I cannot help you find. Nor would I want to. If you choose to die chasing a ghost, Sri Lanka will shed no tear. None remain." Bandula quit.

February 9, 2010

Package came today. Was on the steps, under mangos and rice Bandula has been leaving when I'm gone and running. Corner said Los Angeles. There are pictures of Taprobane online. Michelle must have seen them to accomplish this. It's beautiful. I'm looking off at the setting sun. It's a portrait called "John Durban at the End of the World." Thought maybe they were here. A surprise. Searched the house. It's a miracle anyone could get things so right from so far. Only true love. I want to call her, talk to them. Phone has been ripped from the wall. I am alone. I'll speak out loud. I miss them. I am sorry things turned out like they did in Rio, and in London. So many places. Don't remember me like that, or this. Don't look at me now. The air here is so heavy. I can hardly breathe. Help me. Help.

INSERT SKETCH: "JOHN DURBAN AT THE END OF THE WORLD"

ASIRI HOSPITAL
February 17, 2010

I opened my eyes into the burning ocean, middle of the night, out to sea. I was lured there. Lights were shining in the distance, just beyond Taprobane. Water entering my lungs must have sprung me awake. I could feel the beat of my heart against the black sea. I thought of Burn, of how he would find me washed up, bloated and picked apart by birds on some distant beach, thinking I had missed the point in all of this.

I began to swim for the shore but could make no ground. At some point, before the misunderstanding between us took shape, Bandula explained to me roughly, the tide cycles of southern Sri Lanka. To make it back that day, I would have to fight receding waters until an hour past sunrise, until a new tide would even consider allowing the hope of my return. I kept rotating between dead-man's float and front crawl, knowing that at best, I'd be treading water for hours before any real fight for survival could begin. Every twenty strokes, I'd look up to gauge the distance to shore, to find its lights growing more faint, and ever shifting. Ten minutes could have been an hour, could have been four. Darkness ran the length of everything.

I didn't realize the sun was up until after it was burning me. At a point, I gave up on gauging the land, too tired to lift my head. But I kept moving. I kept breathing, convinced it was a choice to succumb, to remain in control of the fear in my mind, the starvation in my body, or not, for days and days and days, until there was a sharp tug at my ribs. A shock of sensation. An intensifying yank followed. Then another. Same thing happened to my right arm, then my left leg. I thought I was being bit, maybe attacked before I hit my head on something hard and wooden before I lifted out of the water. The salt had burned my sight into a foggy blur. A distant bickering began. I grabbed hold of the long and wooden thing coming up from the ocean floor, and realized I'd swum headfirst into the pole of a stilt fisherman. Others surrounded.

One of the fisherman climbed down to meet me. He shook my head, then poured a bottle of water into my mouth as he unhooked multiple lines from my skin. When he was done, I swam to the nearby shore of Ahangama. When I reached the sand, I laid down in it, to breathe. Then I got up. When I reached the coastline road, I started running the six miles to Taprobane. At some point, I looked down to the gouges in my skin, to the blood escaping my body. I became transfixed. Then, I must've collapsed.

. . .

I was on my way to Taprobane before someone in Sri Lanka began making attempts to contact me. When I got to the hospital, Durban was looking out the window. He must have picked me up out of the corner of his eye because he smiled, grateful and ashamed. He looked small and frail, and his skin was discolored, either stained by the salt or peeling from sunburn. I pulled a chair up to his bed and sat down. He didn't look at me and said, "It's good to see you." The doctor told me after they treated him for dehydration, burns, tetanus and a mysterious form of toxic shock, it was discovered he had been living with a progressively degenerative heart condition. She said her supervisor determined he had likely endured a series of mild heart attacks over the years, and that all attending doctors were left, "Curious of his resilience." He put his head back and closed his eyes. Then, he fell asleep. There was a notebook on his bedside table. I picked it up and opened it to find a drawing Michelle had done for him at our table in Rio. A voice called out from behind me, "You are Sam?" I turned to see a taut and weathered native man in the doorway, watching over the room, as if protecting it. I nodded and stood. We walked outside to keep Durban sleeping. He said, "Your friend is not well. He talks to the dead." When he said it, a chill ran up my spine. I looked back to the bed, to Durban resting peacefully. If it was true, I didn't know what I could do for him, or what anyone could. I wanted to apologize for Durban, or I wanted to say something about the person he really was. But there was nothing I could say. Not right then. I told Bandula I would take care of things from that point. I thanked him for being there. Also, I thanked him for the thousand noble things he probably did that were never acknowledged. He shook my hand, called all of it his duty, and left.

I walked back inside the room, picked up the notebook again. Durban had been writing freehand since we last spent time together in London. It was a thick book and covered in his small, violent scribble, cover to cover. I started from the beginning and read all through the night. It hurt gathering the places he'd been, learning just how detached he had become. Several times, reading his words brought me great fear, great sadness. In the morning he woke and caught me reading. He said with a quiver, "It's possible I'm sick." I stood and hugged him. He hugged me back. I told him I was taking him back to Los Angeles, to get him better. He said, "Okay."

Part Three

LOS ANGELES
June 21, 2010

I had never been to Los Angeles before Burn invited me to come – truly a gaping hole in the repertoire of my world tour. I was immediately impressed by how sprawling and careless and elegant the city seemed to be. Burn's street was called Coldwater. It started in the flatlands of Beverly Hills and then reached up and over the hills of Los Angeles, across Mulholland and then into something else. I remember feeling like he had made it, feeling like he had come so far from when I first met him in Paris, from when he struck me as something else entirely. We were growing up or growing down, depending on how one chose to look at things. I had never accepted anything even remotely close to an offer like the one he had made. I had never gotten one, and even if I had, I would have laughed and or spit in the face of charity like that. Since I recently had problems discerning reality from make believe, Burn insisted the best way to keep me grounded was to include my voice in the collection of all we had done over the recent passage of years and cities. For years, he had been constructing his version of a novel. Including me erased a majority of what he had done. But he was unfazed by that. He said it felt proper, necessary and honest. He did it for me completely, so I would have something tangible to occupy my stay. The gesture meant more than I ever could have imagined.

My driver left me and I walked a path of stairs from the street to their front door. I was standing in front of Burn and Michelle's home. It was perfect. Then I rang the bell and his beautiful girl spotted me through the window. She opened the door and this dog shot out and began circling me, smashing into my legs for attention. Michelle saw me tense from the pure happiness of it all and said something I can't remember that was so delightful. She had a way with words, and a tone that always made me feel welcome. Before we met, I had never really known anything like that. When she pulled me close, to embrace me and thank me for coming, I felt like nothing could ever harm me again. I reached down to touch the dog and told it I would behave civil to it if it would behave civil to me. Michelle told it to sit and it finally chilled out. She told me his name was Payton, named after the American football player from Burn's childhood. I looked to it, spoke its name and asked if we understood each other. Michelle told it to shake. We shook. It seemed we did. Michelle looked mesmerizing and I told her. I was always telling her, long after I dispatched any need to charm the woman, knowing she liked me clearly. Even if she didn't, she would have faked it and marvelously, anything for Burn because that's the kind of girl she is, exquisite and rare. I can't even begin to explain. No justice would be done.

Michelle and I sat on the back porch and had some tea. Burn was out on a job. It was beautiful and quiet in the corner of the world they had created. I confessed I was happy to be there, to spend quality time with the two of them, not recalling a time, ever, when I had understood the concept of quality time. When a pause eventually found us, I asked to see her studio. There is no artist truer than a painter. That's what Burn always said about her, always admiring in others so firmly, the failings he saw within himself. In the corner of the room, a black and white sketch caught my eye. It was hidden beneath a pile of others. All I could see was a fragment and still, I was drawn. It was a work in progress, made obvious by a Polaroid that was taped to the corner of the canvas. She was replicating it, a picture of her and Burn on the beach in South Africa – Boulders Beach. Burn was holding a camera with his arm extended when he took it. There were penguins everywhere. Michelle said she had been working on it

for some time, that she was going to give it to him if they ever had a fight or stopped speaking. Right then I demanded it, because the picture leapt...the look in their eyes, the stroke in her transfer. It was poetry. I was starting in on a second round of pleas when she agreed, told me it would be mine. I kissed her before leading us into a fine daytime drunk.

When I got back to Coldwater, his smell was in the air. John Durban was occupying my home. When I walked inside, everything was quiet. There was an open bottle of wine on the kitchen counter. Dirty dishes and plates were thrown into the sink and had been left out on the table, not cleaned or cleared. Through the back windows, I could see Payton in the sun next to the pool, dead to the world. Durban did it, all of it. It's what he does. I followed music into Michelle's studio, where I found her working under the skylight. She turned and kissed me, told me John had made her lunch before getting a little drunk on two bottles of white. She said he was confessing his life. I asked if he was clean and she said, "Absolutely." He was asleep in the guesthouse and had been for over an hour. It gave me a satisfaction knowing he was there, like one of the clouds hanging over my life had finally departed. She said he was either okay or that he was going to be okay. I can't imagine and have a hard time trying to imagine what John had been through in the months preceding his arrival. Or, in his life. I needed that feeling to end, all of it, for us, for him. We were determined to be there for each other.

It was late at night and I was working when I heard the back door open and a scavenger in the kitchen. I listened as he must've opened every cupboard, then the fridge, then the garage door. He was talking to the dog, negotiating some truce. I heard no less than one dozen dog bones hit the ground. He said good boy and after that I spoke, saying the dog would never leave his side. John put his head around the corner with that smile and said, "Motherfucker...what does a guy gotta do to get a drink around here?"

We took a quick drive to Tower Bar on Sunset. Michelle takes me often to visit the maître d' Dimitri, a Macedonian import, and one of the fine men I've encountered in the city. We have a relationship that goes back to my early days in Los Angeles, when I ran his kitchen for a year. He taught me how to hustle with grace, and to handle myself well in front of icons I grew up admiring. The place is historic and fine like nothing in town. Also, because of Dimitri, it feels forever warm to me. I walked in with Durban and Dimitri put his hands together to welcome us, then bowed into two hugs before stepping back, saying, "Please, please. My friends. Mr. Durban of course. Hello Sam. Yes, yes. Right this way." I took time introducing Durban to people I knew who happened to be there. Some knew of him from my writing, and held a certain reverence that made him uncomfortable. We sat and took our time with the night, probably halfway through the second round when my world seemed to sink in for him. I saw the old look on his face, as his singular spirit finally did reform and take shape. At points in the night, I stood back as he charmed anyone who approached, taking me back to the day we met, to our endless first night about town and inside Ritz Paris. There was certainly renewed lightness about him. I felt like he was experiencing something for the first time, someone else holding the reins. At least he let me believe that.

There were two open seats in a calm, full room – like they had been kept for us. Reminiscent. There was a crowd for a Thursday night, as good as I had seen anywhere, and right down the street from my new home. I was happy about that, happy to be in Los Angeles, riding shotgun next to the life of my friend Burn. I met a lot of artists: directors and writers and musicians and photographers. They wanted to meet me. Burn's writing had created a character John Durban who was received with pity and hatred and lust and fascination, seemingly all at the same time. By the end of the night, I had set up a dozen appointments of

varying degrees across town, beauties to visionaries to literary and cinematic captains of industry. I would attend none.

We picked up a bottle for Mulholland. I told Durban I wanted to show him my city from the sky. There is only one way to see Mulholland for the first time – in a blur. That's what I said before dropping down on the accelerator, before I grabbed and held seventy miles per hour. The first turn was fast approaching and I looked over to John, expecting him to urge me faster. Instead, he was silent. He was uneasy. I dipped speed to fifty going into the first turn, waiting for him to snap back into himself but he never did. When the tires began to rumble and scream, John closed his eyes and his breath stopped. I pulled over to the side of the road and he got out, started to pace with the bottle in his hand, not drinking. I was worried for a moment, like I had done something to set him off until I saw how composed he was, how calm. I realized something important about our past; it belonged there, and I should have known better than to try and bring it back.

He sat up on the hood and started talking. I sat down next to him. He reached inside the car to play "Let Down," and told me he'd listened to it hundreds of times in the past months, "Stuck on emotion." He said it reminded him of things, and settled him. We sat on the hood of the car and he talked about Jenny, mostly of their early days, of falling in love and all the rest. He told me about crashing on the Amalfi coast, speaking of its resemblance to Mulholland. We talked about the power in her stare, the way her body moved, the way she kissed, spoke, laughed, fucked, dreamed. We talked until the sun was coming up, until light started to bend over the hill. He told me he was done crying for her, that the hurt had calmed and had been replaced with something else, something more hopeful. But he wouldn't tell me what that was. He said if he was not fixed from her, truly fixed, he never would have considered bringing himself to Los Angeles and into our lives. Our last Christmas was fast approaching. We let that reality sink in for a moment, somehow undaunted – maybe because we had nearly realized our expression. The love of Durban's life was incapable of living in the world, so she took herself out of it. But he found her. He found her, I found mine, and we found each other.

INSERT SKETCH: DURBAN AND BURN ON HOOD OF CAR MULHOLLAND – VALLEY LIGHTS BELOW

Time glided by. In the mornings, I'd wake up early with Burn and we'd go running. One Sunday, we ran up Coldwater, across Mulholland, down Laurel Canyon and back on Sunset. Burn said it was thirteen miles, and with the hills, even bigger. He once said that running was steel wool scraping away filth in the heart and body. I asked if he was implying that I had filth in my heart and body. He said, "Not like you used to." One morning after a month or so, we got home from an eighteen miler and he told me he was impressed. I felt conditioned and strong. After our runs, we'd sit down and work for a while, which I enjoyed. We had a good time re-living the worlds we roamed, sometimes battling for days over which stories and cities served a purpose and which did not. Every day around 11 AM, when we would finish and when Burn would leave to start his day, I was exhausted. I don't know how he kept going. The man is tireless. Most days, upon Burn's departure and after I'd take Payton down to the park, I'd head up to my room and sleep off the morning. Once awake, I'd stumble downstairs. The dog was always waiting. Sometimes, I'd sit in the backyard to get a tan and just throw a tennis ball against the fence for it to chase over and over. Or I'd spend my afternoons inside, watching Michelle work. At first, it made her uncomfortable but eventually, she would forget I was there. Often, I'd remain until she couldn't paint any longer and we'd head off to find a late lunch at the diner inside of The Beverly Hills Hotel, or at all day breakfast places on Sunset or Beverly or 3rd Street. Or we'd head to the ocean. On occasion and with the day's work behind us, we'd order a bottle of wine, sometimes two and wait for Burn to come and meet us. It was the time of my life.

One day I got a call. Durban and Michelle were around town and wanted me to come meet them. That day he called, not her. The sound in his voice made me ask if everything was okay. Then I had to ask again. All he said was, "You need to get over here." I showed up at a hotel off my old street Holloway, and took a ride up to the roof. They were standing there. She was waiting.

After Burn left, I had a remembrance, a line I had to put into the book. I didn't meet Michelle in her studio that day, didn't watch her work like I always did. Instead, she made her way into the kitchen around 2 and found me working on the computer. She asked what I was doing. There were a million things I could have said to maintain our order and peace, and any one of them would have sufficed. Instead, I told her to read Paris, the day me and Burn met because I found it beautiful and because the three of us had never talked about it to such a depth. At that point, everything was just abstract. There was some minor misbehaving, mostly on my part, but only a little. So, I fell asleep as she read, forgetting. When I woke up, she told me we were leaving. I didn't say a word, not until I called Burn and told him that I had fucked up, and that she might know everything.

Michelle stood and approached. John turned away, walked to the balcony. I thought for a moment he was going to jump. He wouldn't face me, either fearful of me or for me and I hated him for that. She asked what exactly she had read. Berlin. She asked if it was true. Durban had earlier said no, lying. I said no right then. I lied to her face. Tears came into her eyes. She shook them away. I think she knew the truth, though none of us could speak it. She just stood there and strong. She reached for my hand to hold it and said, "I gave you everything." Suddenly, it felt like nothing existed between us.

My back was turned and I could hear the murmur of their voices, vibrations in the air. Then it all stopped. I looked to them. Michelle was sitting on the ground and Burn was kneeling beside her. It was over, the end of the two of them and the three of us, the end of all happiness I had found. I felt myself tearing in two. She reached out and took his hand. Then proposed.

LAS VEGAS
June 24, 2010

Durban rented a big red convertible and we sped the entire route from LA to Vegas, taking turns behind the wheel as Hunter Thompson minus bender. There was lightness in the drive, in the heat rising up from the blazing highway, and in our hearts. Nothing could touch us.

Word around Los Angeles was that Las Vegas was in a downturn. That was very romantic and relatable to me, our invasion of something fleeting, masked with sparkle and bells and whistles, hope and lust, everything as misdirection. We drove all morning through the desert, stopping at Primm for gas and a roller coaster at Buffalo Bill's, the first time, because I was being childish, then again and again and again because they were. There was a sign that said Las Vegas – 39 miles.

We drove past the fountains at The Bellagio and Durban was banging on the car with his fist, saying I want to stay there I want to stay there, not pointing at the hotel, but to the crown structure on top of the roof, which was not available, or eligible. Once inside the hotel, Durban compromised with the team of managers who had been called to assist in his faux outrage, and we ended up in the presidential suite. Even if Durban's funds had dwindled, he still spent recklessly from time to time. He might say otherwise, but he loved Las Vegas. Inside the room, stretching glass windows revealed the strip below us, then eventually the glowing horizon and first cracklings of a neon empire. Michelle told Durban he was ridiculous and he smiled massively, "Best man, love." She said, "Only man."

We split off to different wings. Michelle took a shower and I stepped in, where we made love, easy on the floor as the water fell down from above. She laid over me after, covering my beating body. Her hair was tied in a rope resting warm across my shoulder. She kissed me before getting out and I stayed behind, feeling her echo.

I left ahead of Burn and Michelle to sort things out after taking a quick shower and greasing my head so that I might appear as the great Dean Martin. Then I got into a white tux and left Burn's match next to the airy gown I asked Stella McCartney to make for Michelle, which she agreed upon because the title of my e-mail read, "HUGE favor. Last one, I'll be dead soon!!" I left a note for the engaged, informing them I would be on the floor of the casino and waiting with practiced patience. As grandiose as Las Vegas pretended to be, I was not going to be outdone by it. Not in the time I had left. That's the last thing I was thinking as I checked my reflection in the mirror of the elevator on the way down, sunglasses on, cigarette lit and in hand. When I took just a thin drag, I felt a stab through my heart. My cigarette fell to the floor and my hands fell to my knees. I pulled my sunglasses down, to examine with honesty until I could get no closer, what had become of John Durban. All I had left was determination to see my two dearest wed, show them a night to remember, and then step away, into my last responsibility. When the doors opened, I charged out like a fucking wildling, into the blinding lights and rush, heroically onto the gaming floor.

Michelle and I met John in the lobby and together we floated through. He told us, "Sit back, have faith. Everything has been taken care of." The collective staff, even strangers seemed briefed on the purpose of our visit – all wishing unique luck as we passed. There wasn't a car waiting at the front of the hotel, but three white horses. When I told Durban I'd never been on a horse, he looked to me and said, "Like I fucking have." Michelle was already up and talking to our guide. There was a police escort behind us, a curious crowd, and a handful of people we didn't know who were taking pictures with expensive cameras. Before I could rhetorically ask Durban if he ever thought of his actions as overboard, we were off, trotting Las Vegas Boulevard on horseback, on our way.

We didn't ride long before arriving at a place called El Lil' Chapel. It was true to its name, small and white. We left our horses and approached on the concrete walkway. Plastic hearts and Cupids had been jammed into a cracked bed of scorched soil. Mistletoe hung from the entrance and Durban kissed Michelle. Then he kissed me. We walked inside and were welcomed in Spanish and then poor English by the staff, as the manager expected us to be two consecutive unions from the Oaxacan Benitez family. Durban was oddly furious at the mistake, hastily demanding the services of an English-speaking minister who had left to bail his cousin out of jail and, "No would return for one hour." Durban's negotiations were failing before he stopped to grab hold of his chest and took several slow and careful breaths. I stepped close to him, to hold him up before he shook me off and arose renewed, "We proceed how the world intends!" Durban bought three bottles of Champagne for twenty-eight dollars. None of us drank very far beyond the first toast. We wandered the chapel in line to be wed, but also then in a heated competition to find the best couples' photo among the thousands adorning the walls. We scattered because at some point, Durban was calling me from another room, assuming victory, pointing to '84 Tom and Noelle, a dwarf and giant. Noelle was cradling Tom in her arms like he was her infant child. Game over. We went looking for Michelle, found her standing in front of a photo of her own. Durban was relaying his discovery before he stopped, because our air and hers didn't match, because we were in one world and Michelle was in another, '64 Carlos and Mercedes. Then, '69, '74, '77, '85, '88, '95, '99, '01, '04, '07, and '08. They had been married there twelve times, photos lined left to right, the last of the series revealing them old and gray, surrounded by children and grandchildren. Michelle was studying their faces. She turned to hold me, and settled there, before our names were called through a crackling loudspeaker.

A minister named Felipe stood at the front podium, all nerves because employees had surrounded my description, cabron loco, with other Spanish terms of disrepute. He asked if we were ready, fear-filled, stripping English sentences so bare, all that remained were scarce fragments and wild inflections. To be honest, he was perfect. He was all heart. We spent the entire sermon playing catch up, sentences behind, until he asked them exactly, "So then…to each enough to marry?" I think Burn and Michelle originally intended to exchange some form of vows, but that never happened. Instead, they simply took turns saying yes before they kissed, and were married. Felipe was about to take their picture when Michelle stopped him, refusing unless I also stepped in. That made me very happy. The three of us took a picture none of us saw, by choice, that I like to imagine will remain on the wall of El Lil' Chapel for all eternity. We got back on our horses and set off into the night, trotting a little over two miles down the road, intentionally off the map, still followed by police escort, guide leading the way.

I had solicited the services of a world-renowned chef to cook for us in the desert. When he asked about the menu, I asked for rattlesnake and moonshine. We arrived to find Chef Pedro at work. A picnic table stood atop a patch of watered desert, wrapped in white linen. Four purple roses stood atop the table, cut short and matched to four white candles. Inside each rose bowl was a small current, rippling waves of light. A wood fire burned nearby. There was also a luxury trailer. Once we were seated, Pedro greeted us and laid out expectations for the night. He had also brought along a young Vegas princess to help him serve. She was called Jess, and couldn't have been older than nineteen or twenty. Pedro followed Jess to the table with a large glass jar labeled

"XXX." Jess dropped glasses and moved off as Pedro poured. He told the story about my tracking him down to cook a most bizarre dinner, and how excited he was to soon present it. I thought Burn and Michelle might have paused in the face of my unholy cocktail on the night of their sacred union, but of course they didn't, instead taking it in stride, listening astute and respectfully as Pedro spoke eloquently about how he made the moonshine, infusing it with mild spices that might serve in some way to pair with the rattlesnake. When he said rattlesnake, Michelle laughed out loud and took another sip. Jess brought out three chasers designed to remove splinters from the grain alcohol — grapefruit juice and a touch of cayenne pepper. I asked before or after and Pedro said, "It's one-ninety proof. Like it matters." I waited for Pedro to return with the rattlesnake before toasting the newlyweds, which I did very briefly before we set our heads and throats on fire, before we ate, before Pedro and Jess took their own liberty in bringing out actual and appropriate dishes to line the table. I had bought three bottles of trophy red from the Bellagio's head sommelier but we would never touch them, instead electing small sips of pain while dining under the desert stars. We spent the night laughing at everything. Even after all we'd been through, and against all we knew was coming, happiness is all I can remember when I think back on that night. **Pure joy.**

I'm not sure what Durban would have been had he not been born into what he was born into. Some people, you see straight away — they'll become whatever they want to become. Obstacles shift and move in their presence. He was that. To save the three of our lives, I couldn't have come up with anything even in the realm of what he came up with that night, even before we were riding in the backseat of our arranged 9:30 limo, heading into another unknown. Michelle called up to the driver and asked him to pull over, told us to wait while she stepped outside and returned with her arms full. She handed Durban a gift, large and wrapped. John contested and told her it was bad form to give gifts on the day of one's wedding. Then, he tore through it. It was as if he had never received anything wrapped in his life. I was watching closely as his eyes saw what was inside, and he stopped everything. His hand moved to cradle his chest before he coughed, "That's me. That's us." Michelle had sketched our sitting on the back porch at Coldwater, by the fire, Payton chasing embers in the middle of the night. John was laughing but there were tears. Michelle leaned forward and pulled his forehead to hers, mine to theirs. We remained like that for as for long as we could.

The car stopped and Durban made us put blindfolds on. Everything was overkill, again and as usual with John, but also appropriate. He led us out of the car, through a crowd of voices, then a clanging metal gate. I could immediately feel dirt and a thin glass crunch under every step I took. There was humming, like a swirl of electrical current was moving all around us. As we continued to walk, I could make out the song "Dustland Fairytale." Durban pulled my blindfold. We were standing in the middle of the Neon Graveyard, a place I'd heard about but had never seen, a place where all of the strip's famed signs go when they've burned out. Usually, it was just a daytime tourist trap. That night, it existed as an inferno of endless, beautiful light. Everything was lit up. It must have cost a fortune, or a thousand hours of labor to make it all burn again. The song I heard was being performed by half of the band that created it, a local two man consisting of Dave Keuning and Brandon Flowers. We turned the corner to find them standing in front of us, surrounded by friends, our families, and a couple photographers, playing for a photo shoot and reception that was apparently put together by Benny, who was even standing off to the side and applauding us. Michelle and I were offered congratulations on the song's bridge before the night was brought to life. John was carrying the picture

Michelle had painted under his arm. I didn't think to ask why.

We settled in and listened. I watched Burn and Michelle as they toured and greeted their surprising guests. That was more than enough for me. My head fell back, to pay last respects to the beastly shining stars. I took a deep breath, and exhaled. Then I backed away without goodbye. It hurt so badly, the thought of standing idly by while something existed in this world that was going to destroy us all. It had to be stopped. I had to stop it.

There were notes being played that became "All These Things I've Done," chasing me as I fled. I didn't get far. There was physical pain, brutal and shocking pain that stopped me, forced me to my knees. A life flashed by. I saw my mother's hand from below, tenderness, holding my hand and guiding me through her home, the place she was born. Martinique. I saw her face. The source of my vanity. Cover girl. Abused and abusing. I saw her departure from my life. The devastation. I saw my expulsions, first in the states and then in England. I saw my arrests, my failings and failure to comply with everything, anything laid out before me. I saw raw hatred for the man who was my father. The world. I saw Burn. I saw the way we were, soul mates from the very beginning. I saw us driving through the country in South Africa, Baja, Utah, Big Sur. I saw two funerals. Michelle was sitting alone in the front row for both.

I returned to the night, sweating, dazed, in the dirt, trying to gather the strength to stand. There was a sign in front of me. It was glowing and overpowering. Pulsing. I was paralyzed and staring into it. Time had passed but I didn't know how much. When I finally stood, Burn was standing in front of me. He picked me up.

INSERT SKETCH: DURBAN AND "DEBBIE REYNOLDS" BURN THERE – WHITE TUXEDOS

Durban said, "Look at me, actin' a fool in front of Debbie Reynolds." He saw Michelle standing over my shoulder and asked her to capture it someday, saying, "If I could only ever see myself through your eyes." I knew then Michelle and I were going back to Los Angeles alone. Durban was moving while speaking, apologizing for dropping the painting, trying to clean it, apologizing again, so inconsolable. But determined. He looked over my shoulder to Michelle, "My queen! Guard the kingdom until I return." John looked back to me then, the two of us silent before he slapped my outstretched hand. He hugged me triumphantly, looked into my eyes and didn't need to say another word. He began a theatrical retreat, backpedaling as Michelle moved to my side, as she rested her head on my shoulder. She waved. Durban waved back. He lowered into a waiting cab and was gone.

LOS ANGELES
July 14, 2010

Soon after we returned from Vegas, Michelle drew the portrait Durban had asked of her, his standing in the Neon Graveyard in front of Debbie Reynolds. Then she did them all. With permission from John, she drew fallen Jenny – first in all her glory, then her collapse on the streets of Rio. She drew Paris, Prague, Langa. Everywhere.

When I can't sleep, I watch Michelle. She never moves, so still, so silent. I've never been like that. There's always been something inside of me tossing and turning. I adore her calm, everything she is that I'm not. Sometimes, when we're in bed, she tells me to stop everything I'm doing and feeling and thinking and tells me to just be there with her. Then she rests her head on my stomach, eyes looking up to mine, holding my hand before she says so easy, "Easy now." Her free hand runs across my forehead and through my hair before she says it again, but softer, "Easy." By then, everything has fallen away.

There's a mountain I like to climb that stands about an hour outside Los Angeles. It's a drive through Pasadena and the 210, on the outskirts of a small gem called Mt. Baldy Village. I park at a 5,000-foot landing called San Antonio Falls and start running or walking until I hit the peak, 10,041 feet. In the summer up there, it's empty. Red and blue ski lifts line the first stretches of the hike before the last ascent, Devil's Backbone.

Today, I reached the top, dropped my bag and began to circle. There are valleys, endless, and mountains stretching forever. Civilization is gone. I found the rock that read Mt. San Antonio – 10,041, and took a seat. Michelle approached me that morning. She hadn't been working. I knew because there was no paint or chalk on her face. She asked me to sit before she knelt and took my hand. Then she placed my hand on her stomach and said with a small, fearful smile,

"Sam, I need you to know." My hand began to tremble, then my body. I walked out. I couldn't stay.

The air was cool and still on the mountain. I thought about her life with a son or daughter, without me there, then of that child coming from something broken. Michelle would have to one day explain the choices I had made, and what I had done to myself. I didn't want to imagine what that knowledge could do to something so precious. To hear that. To have to say that. There could be no forgiveness. The person I was is not the person I am today, but saying that now or in the future offers so little. My actions remain. When Michelle was standing in front of me, when all that needed to exist was truth between us, I failed. Then I ran. I ran away, to stand on top of a fucking mountain. Alone.

I started walking east, ashamed of everything I had so revered – empty air and space. Looking down from so high up, I could see a return path bending through trees and rock. My options were to either take three hours and double back on the path I usually came from or save two and cut my own path straight down the face, so I could get back to my car, back to the road, back to my life, back to my girl as quickly as possible. All I could think of was opening the door to find her, so I could tell her I was sorry. Sorry for leaving the way I did. Sorry for everything. I couldn't waste another moment so I stepped off the face, step one into a plunge of Mt. San Antonio. The rocks were steep and jagged. I fell often, immune to pain. I was gaining invincible speed. She filled me then, my Michelle, carrying our child, standing somewhere I wasn't and waiting for my return. I thought of her every step, every breath, descending the mountain in bold leaps, as blood turned to black stone across my body.

The highway was oddly empty by the time I got back. I looked into the mirror and needed stitches. There was a flap of skin hanging loose from my face that would shake up and down across bumps in the road. I could feel the eyes of drivers as I passed them, gawking my appearance through the window by way of faint light. There was a precise moment on the ride home. New certainty. I could no longer accept what I had done. I needed to see the million things I'd not seen. I needed to stay. I needed to be someone's husband, son, friend. I needed to be someone's father.

I pulled into Coldwater around nine. When I got inside, Payton approached me, barking before hearing my voice, thinking I was some intruder. Michelle wasn't home. I always knew. There was a bag from Dan Tana's and a note next to it with a drawn heart. I was starving but not hungry, and looked at the bag before thinking about where she could be and how I might find her. I started a shower. The house felt empty. I imagined my life like that, empty without her. Lost. I imagined the return of all weakness she so gracefully swept away. The water was covering my skin, stinging, washing clean. My head hung low as I watched a mix of blood and dirt pour from my body, swirl against tile and flow down the drain. I felt I was about to shatter when her arms wrapped me from behind. Her head fell against my back and I felt the press of her clothed body. We stood there under the water until I spoke. I told her we would be okay as long as it turned out like her. Then I said I was never going to leave her. She turned me around and ran her thumb across the split in my brow, sealing it.

INSERT SKETCH:
MICHELLE AND BURN IN THE SHOWER
MICHELLE IN CLOTHES

I recently met Alexandr in Zanzibar. He seemed to be hiding. Or, he needed to be hiding our meeting. He had sent word, the only word left I cared about. He was sitting in front of an empty bottle in the middle of the day. At some point he said, "Life is too short to keep enemies." He told me there was good news, and bad news. The bad news choked him up a bit. He said, "I cannot help you." I was somehow ready for that, clearly more than he was. He had to compose. Then he began, "You can possibly help your friend." What came next was his best and only move, and there would be no guarantees. He told me when it came to our unbreakable exit, there were two lists, Viktor and Sophia, named after the originating Orlov lovers. Viktor was *kill*, Sophia was *be killed*. Burn and I were Sophia. Somehow, Alexandr was able to hack me onto the Viktor list, meaning I had adopted a new occupation. He said I would need to be in the Seychelles on the tenth of September. After the tenth of September, if everything went according to plan, I would remain a Viktor. Then, it would become possible for me to receive Burn's contract, and simply let it pass. Alex was confident he could cover the rest.

Emilio Santos rented a small house on the water, in paradise. He grew a beard and his hair, got fat and paid everything in cash under a false name. The island was located about 40 miles from Mahe. On it, there were a couple small hotels and a few hundred locals. Visitors I met in bars seemed to all be newlyweds, all glowing from the sun and overload fucking. The place was picturesque and peaceful.

I spent the first few days following him around the island. His schedule was always the same. In the mornings, he would wake around 8, then walk to his porch for calisthenics of jumping jacks, push-ups and toe touches. He would then take his fishing pole and tackle box out to the water, where he would fish for hours, often until noon. I'd sit on the sand nearby, by other couples for ambiguity, drinking Kilimanjaro and getting a tan as he cast and reeled, cast and reeled. Every half-hour or so, he would hook something worth keeping. At the end of the day, he would walk the catch, which was always substantial, to a small restaurant at the edge of the road. At noon or 1, he would return to his home for the afternoon, often reading on the porch until he fell asleep. I spent a lot of time in the sun, on the sand, waiting for my nerve to arrive and the day to come. Around sundown, Emelio would go inside, clean himself up and saunter to the roadside restaurant with a bottle of wine in hand, where an old local played the piano and a cook would serve up his catch. After the second night, I started going inside. It was a small place, but when darkness fell, the tables would swell with couples, few locals and the two of us. Every night around 9, he would leave a generous tip and retreat back to his porch, where he would smoke and listen to *Grand Hotel* or *Blood on the Tracks* or *Houses of the Holy*. At 11, he would slip inside to retire. Morning after morning, I watched him wake and do it all over again.

The last night I spent on the island, I was sitting at the bar when he sat down next to me. He ordered a bottle of rum and two glasses. When it came he poured one for himself and then a second before sliding it to me. He spoke in a very deep and sensual voice, "Salud." My breath shortened. We touched glasses and looked into each other's eyes. He said, "I have seen you walking the beaches and in the restaurant. You are not here with a woman?" I shook my head. He said, "A young man like you. You should be here with a woman. Sometimes there are women here without husbands. Sometimes there are women with husbands who need to feel like they haven't a husband. But you musn't fuck the locals. Whatever you do. It upsets the dichotomy." As hard as I tried to make no connection, a smile appeared, which he used as a sign that he could get closer to me. I thought over and over to excuse myself, to remove myself from the situation before I began to see him as a living, bleeding, thinking, feeling thing. I knew the importance of detachment and still failed. Our first drink turned to several. I tried again to create some form of elaborate distaste, but couldn't. He was clumsy and funny. He invited me to his table. There, we talked about the parts of Buenos Aires he missed most. His poignant words were steeped in regret, about a family he once had, and a lover. He made me promise to visit the city someday, to come across his wife, Barella Santos. He said to me, "While I have many regrets, she was never one of them. Tell her that." I couldn't possibly make that promise, and yet I did. It seemed such an absurd request until I began to catch up. He was steps ahead. If he had thought to run to such a remote island, he must have also thought to develop awareness for things he should be running from, like a perfectly timed stranger with an odd, uneasy linger.

We walked back to his house, where he lit several lanterns on the porch. He pulled a record and started *Exile on Main Street*. Then he disappeared inside before returning with another bottle of rum. By then he was getting sloppy. We both were. He pulled a joint and lit it. We smoked it pass by pass until it was gone. After that, we both sat back. Any formalities that should have existed between us had been stripped bare. My head fell. He leaned forward to steady my shoulder. When I looked up, he was holding an antique pistol and pointing it right at me. I took a breath and waited for him to pull the trigger. He said, "I never knew what it meant to live a good life. Things I should have cherished I did not. Not until I knew you were coming.

Perhaps that's the idea." He turned the barrel on himself and handed me the gun. I took it but shook my head. I couldn't, not that way. There was humanity left in me after all.

I thought of telling him about Burn and Michelle, about their kid and how his death was going to serve something great, and noble. But then I couldn't. We reached a moment where silence took hold. He stood, stepped down off the porch and onto the sand. I stood and followed. Ahead in the water, a strip of moonlight was being drawn to us. He was walking right into it. I followed him out. He began singing a Spanish lullaby as his feet entered the water. I was close behind him when he stopped and knelt, singing until I swung the pistol against his head and he fell into the crashing water. He floated on top of the surface for a moment, flowing over the waves before I held him in my arms, took him under and kept him. I expected a struggle. None came. After enough time had passed, I lifted his body and pulled it to shore. Then, I pulled him into his house. Then, onto his bed. His blood crawled across the pillows and white sheets. Music had stopped playing on the porch. The needle was scratching.

The following is transcribed from paper Sam Winburn was writing on in Barcelona beneath a storm. Some words have faded or bled together. Assumptions have been made in parenthesis.

September 29, 2010

I'm going to be a father. I'm not sure anything else has ever mattered. I'm going to be a (father). I've never been so afraid of anything as much as her, my coming daughter. My little girl. She's coming to remove everything damaged in me. I'm going to be a father. I can't stop saying it. Thinking it. Feeling. I need to (stop) time and keep her away, so I can remain. I need her here now, to touch her, to hold her, speak to her, to see Michelle in her. To tell her that I love her.

Today walked La Rambla to the harbor as the sun was setting. Found a spot on the bench. Watched the day (move), (the gondolas stretch) high above the city, people through the (walkways across the lawns and heat). (Life) rules this place. Everywhere I go, I can't escape. I'm sitting in front of the harbor now, done watching the pink sky turn red to purple to gray to black. The winds are growing, kicking up the streets. The world runs for (cover). I cannot see a single star in the sky. Getting colder. Garbage stirs at my feet — (branches), leaves.

My feet dig into the cold (sand). The first drop of rain touches my skin. Billions follow. The rain (tastes) sweet. Lightning reveals the sky, folds of cloud ready to descend upon and bury the world. (Vast). Thunder shakes me. I envision setting sail into (the) sea, on boat, rolling above the (waves). Their great and powerful heights. I can see (the one to conquer me), to tip me and take me under — ending this. Instead, lightning (strikes and freezes) the sea, turning it to endless marble, (spilling) me out of my boat, across it, (sparing). A miracle. From there, I'll be allowed to sit, to marvel the gift of life, to toe the line I toed and survive.

The clouds clear. The (sky) is scorched by an army of stars. The world stands before me now and I know four things. I'm going to be a father to a daughter. I miss Michelle. Durban is coming. We will find a way.

162

BARCELONA
September 30, 2010

For the first time in my life, I was waiting for Burn. I had picked a bar that wasn't far from the harbor, but don't recall the name or location. Never will. The place was dark, everything painted black or deeply stained. I was sipping something sweet, lost on how I'd tell him of what had been done and what remained without him throwing a fucking fit. He said he had something to tell me too, something he couldn't say over the phone. Things felt strangely off between us, and in the spaces surrounding us. That was the other thing. Looking back, I felt it. It was all so clear.

He glided in, heart bursting. I saw him and leapt. We crossed the room and met with an embrace before he slapped me so hard across the cheek, people turned to look. They were always turning to look. We were different. We brought the best out of each other. Elevated each other's existence. I know that. We grabbed a seat at a table by the bar, split by the light of a flickering candle. Over four years, Burn had never told me anything that came with so much hesitation or preface. I asked straight away. He smiled the way Burn does, cool before he said exactly, "I'm going to be a dad. It's a baby girl." Looking back now, I try to imagine how my reaction appeared to him in the moment, hoping I came off the way I felt, saved and enamoring. I could not see another man more fit to raise a child in this world. I told him this and then said something even grander about Michelle as a mother, which was also true. He broke into a laugh so wild and careless, I watched it from start to finish. I couldn't stop saying it out loud – Burn, you're going to be a dad. There was such power behind those words. We raised a glass then drank, hardly drinking. He spoke of dreams, the four of us running to the ends of the Earth. I listened, urged him to talk, to exhaust every last hope and fear, knowing exactly what he was talking about. At the end of the night and with nothing left to say, I would give him my gift. He would see his daughter born, and watch her thrive. He would grow old with Michelle, and have a family. He would be free.

It was sometime after 9 when we met, originally agreeing to find each other for a drink before wandering town. Suddenly, it was 11, then after midnight. We did a second shot, Jack for old times. Our souls were fine by that, reflective, beyond bad ends of bottles and towns. We were aged and not, tamed and yellowed and frayed. Still so young. We looked at each other and spoke to each other that night with pride. We agreed on being fortunate, even through the hard times, to call such lives ours. I keep telling myself this now, in writing, over and over. We were lucky. That was true. It needs to be true.

It was past 1 when a small crowd appeared. They had arrived around us, just kids. I'm twenty-nine, I've earned the right to label youth, especially as the night began to take them over. We were in a high-end bar in a high-end district of Barcelona. The line should have been drawn at the door. They should not have been there. We had a waitress, pure and delicate named Petra. She was twenty-one and recently cut by something. That was Burn's thought. He said, "Aren't we all. All the time. But we're something else now, aren't we?" At a point, he was following her across the room with his eyes, protecting her as she walked her rounds. When she came back to us, Burn asked what she was studying and what she wanted to be. She told him everything he wanted to hear. She asked about his wedding ring. He told her about the edges of South Africa, of finding Michelle there, and how she was pregnant with their first child. He told her about his plans to build them a home, somewhere on a hidden coast, where he and his family could count sunsets forever. Every word left him with such lightness. Petra loved him for it. I loved him always. He was so right, about it all. In four years, we had become so much. We had become something else.

Another hour passed and still, I couldn't summon the nerve to tell him. I wasn't ready. At the bar, three guys started to cause a minor scene around Petra. I could see something happening through the corner of Burn's eye. Every time they were on her, he was fighting to bury himself, parts of himself that had been put away. Petra was there reluctantly that night, covering the shift for a sick friend. That's what she told us early on, before she got busy and then harassed, before I saw Burn turning inside. He once told me his process of thought, "When I see someone good taking on unnecessary evil, I imagine them as the person I love most. That way I'll always do what's right." His eyes kept moving to the bar. I felt his pulse rising until I couldn't help but try and steer him away. I knew he was seeing Michelle, but then also the child she was carrying, their child. I saw the look in his eyes. If Lucifer were stirring the bar that night, Burn would have met him. Just as he began to stand, just as he said, "Just a word," just as I pleaded for him to stay put, the crowd was leaving. Then they were gone. Petra came back to our table. She said they were saying awful things. She asked them to leave several times but the bar's bouncer had called out sick. She said, "You wouldn't believe what I endure." I saw veins bulge on the side and front of Burn's head. She saw them too, and assured him everything was okay. When Burn calmed, I asked Petra where we could find something good to eat. She told us about her favorite place in the city, then drew a map and said, "Ask for Benecio. If you're still there when I get there, we'll talk some more." Then she turned and walked away. I asked Burn what was next. He winked and said, "We go ask for Benecio." Then he got up and moved to the bathroom.

Burn's phone began to light. It was Michelle. I picked it up, told her I loved her and that her boys were behaving. Her voice was flat, nothing behind it. She told me she needed to call, to check in. Then she said something I'll never forget, "As long as he's with you John…as long as he's with you." Out the corner of my eye, I could see the bar was moving again. The sight unseated me. I looked to the bathroom and stood to move, to find Burn. The crowd had returned, and were surrounding Petra again. Burn was already there. I asked Michelle to hold on, said I had to go rescue her man. I put the phone in my front shirt pocket. The whole world was hers to hear.

Petra was standing a short distance away, looking on next to Burn, then to me and not calm. I moved closer, to a divider that was separating us, on high ground with a ready bottle in my hand. Burn had everything under control. He mostly always did. Most people immediately wanted to befriend him, not fight him. He had a way. He could take someone apart from the inside without ever being offensive or invasive. That's what he was in the midst of, navigating some gentle rationale I couldn't hear. The three or four boys were just watching him, their eyes like ice. I could see and feel the energy of the room swirling before everyone cracked a smile and Burn seemed to have won. I eased up. Whatever peace he needed to speak to find peace within himself was nearing an end. I took a seat on the closest stool I could find and pulled Michelle back out, long enough to ask her if she was still there. Suddenly, the room exploded in movement. I looked up to the crowd dispersing, rushing out. I told Michelle to hold on before putting her away again, as Petra's eyes found mine, distressed and summoning and I couldn't know why. Burn was standing there, alone at the bar. I jumped the divider. His eyes slowly dragged the room, searching for something, for someone…like he was lost or…then he saw me and didn't move. I walked to him, found him weightless and asked what was up because one of us had to say something. He just stood there. The music was loud. I could feel Michelle calling my and Burn's name from my pocket when Petra approached and took Burn's cheek into her hand, looked into his eyes. She asked him what was wrong. He said nothing. I turned him to face me, to put my hands on his shoulders, to shake him. I'd never seen sadness like that. The music was fucking loud, too fucking loud. I had to get him out of there. I took a hold of his shirt. The fabric was warm. It was already soaked through when he fell to the floor. I screamed for help.

The ambulance arrived quickly. Burn had two puncture wounds, one in his abdomen and the other in his lower back. His skin was exposed and covered in blood. The paramedics were doing everything they could to look concerned and protect his life. He was calm, holding my hand. He said, "I can't believe it. Not yet." I apologized that I wasn't right there as I wiped blood from his chest and abdomen, to keep his body clean, to protect him from further harm. I finally told him he didn't have to run, or worry anymore, or ever again. I had found us a way out, and told him Alexandr was our boy now. He laughed at the last part, probably as hard as he could have before he began shaking, before he looked up to say, "Fuck Johnny, I'm gonna die." I insisted he wasn't, and that he just hold on. It was one hundred and forty minutes past midnight. His blood was rolling on the floor of our Spanish ambulance. The two paramedics were boiling into something of a fever pitch but I couldn't pay attention to that, because I realized something then, how important it was to stop everything I was doing and thinking and assuring and just be there, in those moments, with my friend. We always promised that no matter the state of the world around us, we would conduct ourselves well, that we would live through all moments with dignity and grace. It was the last thing we talked about before I told him I believed we had. He looked to me, nodded in agreement before the strangest thing happened. His eyes slowly closed and his grip fell loose. Then Burn died.

The ambulance eventually came to a stop. They pulled him away. I watched from outside as he was wheeled into the hospital. I stood there and waited for the world to take back what had happened. It never did. The paramedics were pushing Burn's body through a glass hallway but their haste was gone. Michelle was crying in my pocket.

EDITOR'S NOTE

Rumors of Sam Winburn's death began to circle our offices in New York on the morning of October 1st. The following is the first official print article, taken from *La Vanguardia* in Barcelona. It has been translated.

"Visiting Writer Killed In Bar Dispute"
October 1, 2010

Sam Winburn, 29, a journalist and writer from Los Angeles, died early Sunday morning after suffering two stab wounds during a bar altercation. He was rushed to the Hospital De Sant Pau where he was confirmed DOA.

Suspects Pedro Almodar and Errio Norale, 20 and 23, were found and arrested shortly after the altercation and have been charged with murder.

Winburn spent his brief career documenting the arts, and travel. He also developed a following for his work documenting the life of his companion John Durban and the life of his wife Michelle. He was with John Durban when the attack took place.

LOS ANGELES
October 4, 2010

Michelle flew to Spain to meet me. There and together, we answered questions and filled out paperwork and survived. She didn't cry, not once the entire time she was in the city. It made me think her and Burn had discussed this exact thing happening, that they had spent hundreds of hours in the middle of his sleepless nights finding some form of understanding about the meaning of life or about how they would behave if this hand we were dealing with ever became the hand we were dealt. She was so together. I don't remember eating, or thinking, or breathing for the two days we spent in Barcelona. At some point towards the end Michelle looked at me and said, "I don't want to go home. All of this new again." She asked if I understood. I told her I did.

Before flying home, we agreed to turn his body to ashes. Michelle took him through airport security as a carry on. By then, some people knew of who we were and of what had happened. Random pictures were being taken. When we got to the gate and were waiting for the flight, I asked Michelle if she would be okay if I went to the bathroom. She said yes. I looked to my watch, the first time we had been apart in forty hours. In the bathroom, I found my reflection in the mirror. My eyes were dark and sunken. My skin was pale. I hadn't shaved in days, or slept, and I remember thinking at least there was honestly in that, having no desire to cure or form an appearance.

I returned to Michelle at gate nine as she was standing and looking out the window. I sat across the way, away from her. The sun was just starting to fall. A wild glow swept across her face and revealed tears dripping off her chin. Without the light, I never would have seen – the way she intended, thinking it necessary to provide me that illusion of strength. I don't know why. She wasn't blinking or moving, just still as they fell. I wanted to move to her but knew I shouldn't. We sat for the next hour on opposite sides of the gate, as the plane was delayed once then again, as we remained crying and apart. I have no explanation for that.

...

The memorial was held somewhere in Beverly Hills, at the sprawling home of someone Burn was associated with in some way. I don't know who put it together, but it was big and there were pictures of him all over. I was in some and Michelle was in some and the rest were up to feed the animals. I kept my eye on Michelle, watching her move through the grounds with strength to spare. I was mostly alone, putting in my time, wandering when I came across Burn's parents. We had never met but knew each other right away. I moved into them, approaching with great care before mentioning he was his mother and father's son, that I could see it from across the lawn. His father didn't move, very stoic. There was a long silence before his mother took my hand and smiled – Burn's smile – before saying she had enjoyed hearing of our adventures together. We stood together for minutes with nothing to say. That didn't matter. Nothing mattered. His father put his hand on my shoulder and held it hard. I looked to him, into his sad eyes. He said, "Anything you need from now on, please let us know."

At some point, I approached Benny at the back bar. He was holding a martini. Then with bloodshot eyes he said, "I never thought it would actually come to this. Never. He became my friend too." We talked about the word legacy and how it would pertain to Burn. I told him I was done writing, almost, that I was going to finish this last chapter and then leave everything behind. It would be up to him to present correctly. I had already taken the binder that contained everything, and sent it to his office in New York. Michelle agreed to turn in her drawings when she became able to. Benny said, "I will deliver it well. You have my word."

There was a microphone. At some point, people started making their way towards it. I listened to them talk about how his life and theirs intersected. They offered remembrances from noon until I could no longer understand words. Some barely knew him, but that was enough. A similar theme emerged from his dear friends. They spoke of him as some vague thing they were never allowed to fully see. It was strange. He wasn't like that at all. Michelle took the microphone around 2 to thank everyone for coming. She had nothing else to say. When that became clear, I felt the heavy stench of expectation move to me. They were all waiting. Next thing I knew, my body was walking up to the platform. I passed Michelle. She stopped me, to look into my eyes. She lifted my hand between us, held it hard and said, "What about you, John? What about you?" My silence moved her to sit. I had nowhere to go, so I continued, stepping onto the platform, taking the microphone. When I looked up, I caught the eyes that were on me – all of them at once. For a good minute, I paced with nothing to say, lost and scared and hurt. I thought about what they wanted, what they needed. They needed me to drive his stake into the ground, to mark his life but that wasn't my job. He had already done that himself.

TRANSCRIBED:

I don't know what I'm doing here, up here, here at all. I met Burn four years ago under the Eiffel Tower because I was looking to get laid. Not by him. See, when I met Burn, I was something of an addict for all the wrong kinds of things. I was in trouble. Though to be fair, not everything has changed.

-- John stops. He looks to a photo of Burn.

The night we met, we had a night. Where's Naomi?

-- John looks into the crowd. He points.

My God, there you are. I didn't think you'd be here. So many people here. You know, without you, who knows? Every little thing leads us to the next little thing. Eventually, it all adds up. Right? I mean, not long after you came and went, me and Burn made something of a pact. We were both twenty-five and knew nothing of what we wanted, only that we wanted to conquer the world or be conquered by it, to spend every day chasing pursuits worthy of discourse, to push our lives past the point of rupture. Looking back, I have to believe we did. Or else, what have we done? We were always meant to die young.

-- John stops. The crowd begins to stir, upset and confused. Some walk out.

Burn. You were an armored warrior. Yet such a heart. I watched the power it had over you, to take you apart and bring you back. Michelle, when he found you his old world ended and another began. You know that. Thank you for allowing me to borrow time in your lives. It has meant more to me than...anything I've ever been a part of.

-- John stops. He wipes his face, shakes his head. He is flustered.

I can't put into words exactly what happened over the last four years. But, if I could stand before myself, the day before we met, I'd say chin up, something good is coming. That's what Burn was to me. I'm better because of him. This is as good as I'll ever be.

-- John stops.

I don't know where I'm going now. None of this really matters anymore. I'm supposed to be alive for another...eighty days? When you come to understand

why, which you will, a great many of you will wish I had offered some form of repentance here. You'll wish I told you it was wrong for us to live the way we lived, wrong for us to believe the things we believed. We weren't wrong.

-- John looks to Michelle. Points to her. His voice cracking. **Call her Burn and let her be exactly like her father.**

-- John moves to the sound system.

-- A song plays: "Leave Before the Lights Come On."

-- John turns up the volume until it's very loud.

-- John picks up the urn holding Burn's ashes, kisses it.

-- John moves to Michelle.

-- John and Michelle kiss and embrace.

-- John says something into Michelle's ear, touches her stomach. Speaks to it.

-- John walks to the back gate, and exits.